BENEATH
THE BANNER

BEING NARRATIVES OF NOBLE LIVES
AND BRAVE DEEDS

F. J. CROSS

1st WORLD
LIBRARY
Literary Society

Beneath The Banner

F. J. Cross

© 1st World Library – Literary Society, 2004
PO Box 2211
Fairfield, IA 52556
www.1stworldlibrary.org
First Edition

LCCN: 2004091185

Softcover ISBN: 1-59540-631-X
eBook ISBN: 1-59540-731-6

Purchase *"Beneath The Banner"*
as a traditional bound book at:
www.1stWorldLibrary.org/purchase.asp?ISBN=1-59540-631-X

1st World Library Literary Society is a nonprofit
organization dedicated to promoting literacy by:

- Creating a free internet library accessible from any computer worldwide.
- Hosting writing competitions and offering book publishing scholarships.

Readers interested in supporting literacy
through sponsorship, donations or
membership please contact:
literacy@1stworldlibrary.org
Check us out at: www.1stworldlibrary.org

Beneath The Banner
contributed by the Mahaney Family
in support of
1st World Library Literary Society

CONTENTS.

BENEATH THE BANNER.

STORIES OF MEN AND WOMEN WHO HAVE BEEN STEADY WHEN "UNDER FIRE".

ONLY A NURSE GIRL!

THE STORY OF ALICE AYRES.

On the night of Thursday, 25th April, 1886, the cry rang through Union Street, Borough, that the shop of Chandler, the oilman, was in flames.

So rapid was the progress of the fire that, by the time the escapes reached the house, tongues of flame were shooting out from the windows, and it was impossible to place the ladders in position. The gunpowder had exploded with great violence, and casks of oil were burning with an indescribable fury.

As the people rushed together to the exciting scene they were horrified to find at one of the upper windows a girl, clad only in her night-dress, bearing in her arms a child, and crying for help.

It was Alice Ayres, who, finding there was no way of escape by the staircase, was seeking for some means of preserving the lives of the children in her charge. The frantic crowd gathered below shouted for her to save herself; but that was not her first aim. Darting back into the blinding smoke, she fetched a feather-bed and forced it through the window. This the crowd held whilst she carefully threw down to them one of the children, which alighted safe on the bed.

Again the people in the street called on her to save her own life; but her only answer was to go back into the fierce flames and stifling smoke, and bring out another child, which was safely transferred to the crowd below.

Once again they frantically entreated her to jump down herself; and once again she staggered back blinded and choking into the fiery furnace; and for the third time emerged, bearing the last of her charges, whose life also was saved.

Then, at length, she was free to think of herself. But, alas! her head was dizzy and confused, and she was no longer able to act as surely as she had hitherto done. She jumped - but, to the horror of that anxious admiring throng below, her body struck against the projecting shop-sign, and rebounded, falling with terrific force on to the hard pavement below.

Her spine was so badly injured that although everything possible was done for her at Guy's Hospital, whither she was removed, she died on the following Sunday.

Beautiful windows have been erected at Red Cross Hall, Southwark, to commemorate her heroism; but the best memorial is her own expression: "I tried to do my best" - for this will live in the hearts of all who read of her self-devotion. She had tried to do her best *always*. Her loving tenderness to the children committed to her care and her pure gentle life were remarked by those around her before there was any thought of her dying a heroic death. So, when the great trial came, she was prepared; and what seems to us Divine unselfishness appeared to her but simple duty.

F. J. Cross

A SLAVE TRADE WARRIOR.

SOME STORIES OF SIR SAMUEL BAKER.

Sir Samuel Baker, who died at the end of the year 1893, aged seventy-three, will always be remembered for the splendid work he did in the Soudan during the four years he ruled there, and for his explorations in Africa.

In earlier life he had done good service in Ceylon, had been in the Crimea during the Russian war, and had superintended the construction of the first Turkish railway.

Then, at the age of forty, he turned his attention to African travel. Accompanied by his wife, he left Cairo in 1861; and, after exploring the Blue Nile, arrived in 1862 at Khartoum, situated at the junction of the White and Blue Nile. Later on he turned southward. In spite of the opposition of slave owners, and without guide or interpreter, he reached the Albert Nyanza; and when, after many perils, he got safely back to Northern Egypt, his fame as an explorer was fully established. His was the first expedition which had been successful in penetrating into Central Africa from the north. On his return to England he was welcomed with enthusiasm, and received many honours.

In the year 1869, at the request of the Khedive of Egypt, Sir Samuel undertook a journey to the Soudan to put down the slave trade.

He was given supreme power for a period of four years. In December, with a small army of about 1500 men, he left Cairo for Gondokoro, about 3000 miles up the Nile, accompanied by his wife. It was a terrible journey. His men fell ill, the water in the river was low in many places, and the passage blocked up. At times he had to cut channels for his ships; the men lost heart; and, had the leader not been firm and steadfast, he would never have reached his destination.

On one occasion he found his thirty vessels stranded, the river having almost dried up. Nothing daunted, he cut his way through a marsh, making a progress of only twelve miles in about a fortnight. At the end of this time he found it was impossible to proceed further along that course, and had to return to the place he had left and begin again.

Still, in spite of all obstacles, he made steady progress.

At Sobat, situated on the Nile above Khartoum, he established a station, and had a watch kept on passing ships to see that no slaves were conveyed down the river.

One day a vessel came in sight, and keeping in the middle of the river would have passed by without stopping. But Sir Samuel, having his suspicions aroused, sent to inspect it.

The captain declared stoutly he had no slaves aboard. He stated that his cargo consisted simply of corn and ivory. The inspector was not convinced, and determined to test the truth of this statement. Taking a ramrod, he drove it into the corn. This produced an answering scream from below, and a moment later a woolly head and black body were disclosed. Further search was made, and a hundred and fifty slaves were discovered packed as close as herrings in a barrel. Some were in irons, one was sewn up in a sail cloth, and all had been cruelly treated.

Soon the irons were knocked off and the poor slaves set free, to their great wonder and delight.

Sir Samuel arrived at Gondokoro on the 15th of April, 1871. Already two years of his time had expired. In addition to checking the slave trade, he had been commissioned to introduce a system of regular commerce. He set to work at once to show the people the benefits of agricultural pursuits. He got his followers to plant seeds, and soon they were happy enough watching for the green shoots to appear.

But before long they began to suffer from want of food. The tribes round about had been set against them by the slave hunters, and would supply them with nothing; so that Baker, in the midst of plenty, seemed likely to perish of starvation. However, he soon adopted energetic measures to prevent that. Having taken official possession of the land in the name of the Khedive he seized a sufficient number of animals for his requirements.

The head man of the tribe and his followers were soon buzzing about his ears like a swarm of wasps; but seeing he was not to be frightened by their threats they showed themselves ready enough in the future to supply him with cattle in return for payment.

His own soldiers were nearly as troublesome as the natives. They were lazy and mutinous; the sentries went to sleep, the scouts were unreliable, they were full of complaints; whilst round about him were the natives, ready to steal, maim, and murder whenever they could get an opportunity.

His life was daily in danger; and, so as not to be taken unawares, he organised a band of forty followers for his personal service. On these men he could always rely. They were proud of the confidence placed in them, and were ready to go anywhere and do anything. By a strange perversity they were nicknamed "the forty thieves," though they were amongst the very few who were honest.

What with sickness and fighting and losses encountered on the way up the river, Baker's force was now reduced to about five hundred men, in place of the twelve hundred whom he had once reviewed at Gondokoro. Still, he did not despair of accomplishing, with God's help, the mission on which he had been sent.

In January, 1872, with his wife and only two hundred and twelve officers and men, he started south on a journey of three or four hundred miles into the region where the slave trade was carried on with the greatest activity.

He had arranged with one of the chiefs to supply him with two thousand porters to carry the goods of the expedition; but when the time came not a single man was forthcoming. So his soldiers had to be their own carriers for a time. At a later date he was enabled to hire five hundred men to assist him to transport his goods, and presented each with a cow as a reward for his services. All took the cows readily enough, but sixty-seven of the carriers did not appear at the time appointed. The others were extremely desirous of going to look after them; but Baker, knowing their ways full well, thought it better to lose the services of the sixty-seven men rather than to allow this; for he felt sure if they once returned to search for their companions there would be no chance of seeing a single one of them again.

After many perils he reached the territory of Kabbu Rega on the Victoria Nile. The king was apparently friendly at first. But on several occasions the war drums sounded, and although no violence was actually offered yet Sir Samuel thought it well to be on his guard.

He therefore set his men to work to build a strong fort. They cut thick logs of wood, and planted them firmly in the ground, prepared fireproof rooms for the ammunition, and were in the course of a few days ready in case of emergency.

These preparations had been made none too soon.

A few days later a very strange thing happened. The king sent Sir Samuel a present of some jars of cider. This he gave to his troops. A little while afterwards one of his officers rushed in to say the men had been poisoned.

It was really so. The men who had drunk of the cider were lying about in terrible pain, and apparently dying.

At once Sir Samuel gave them mustard and water and other emetics, and they were soon better. But he knew that trouble was at hand.

Next morning he was standing at the entrance to the fort with one of his men when a chorus of yells burst upon his ear. He told his bugler to sound the alarm, and was walking towards the house to get a rifle when the man beside him fell shot through the heart.

The fort was surrounded by thousands of natives, who kept up a continuous fire, and the bushes near at hand were full of sharp-shooters. But the fort was strong, and its defenders fought bravely; the woods were gradually cleared of sharp-shooters, and the natives, ere long, broke and fled.

Then Sir Samuel sent a detachment out of the fort, and set fire to the king's divan and to the surrounding huts to teach the people a lesson for their treachery.

But the place was full of foes. A poisoned spear was thrown at Sir Samuel, and every day he remained his force was in danger of destruction, so he determined to go on to King Riongo, whom he hoped would be more friendly.

It is wonderful that the party ever got there. First of all it was found that they would probably be a week without provisions; but, happily, Lady Baker had put by some supplies, and great was the rejoicing when her forethought became known.

Then it was discovered that the country through which they had to pass was full of concealed foes. From the long grass and bushes spears were constantly hurled at

F. J. Cross

them, and not a few of the men were mortally wounded. Sir Samuel saw several lances pass close to his wife's head, and he narrowly escaped being hit on various occasions.

But, at last, Riongo's territory was reached. The king was friendly, and for a time they were in comparative safety.

By April, 1873, Baker had returned to Gondokoro, and his mission ended. It was, to a great extent, the story of a failure, so far as its main purpose was concerned, owing to the opposition of the men who were making a profit by dealing in slaves; and who, whilst appearing to be friendly, stirred up the natives to attack him. But, failure though it was, he had done all that man could do; and the expedition stands out as one of the most glorious efforts which have been made against overwhelming odds to put an end to the slave trade.

TWO WORKING MEN HEROES.

THE STORY OF CASE AND CHEW.

The large gasholders, which are often a source of wonder to youthful minds as they rise and fall, are the places in which gas is stored for the use of our cities.

By day, when they are generally receiving more gas than they are giving out, they rise; and again at night, when less is being pumped into them than is going out for consumption in the streets and houses, they fall. The gasholder is placed in a tank of water, so that there is no waste of gas as the huge iron holder fills or empties.

Now it was in one of these gasholders that a few years ago two men did a deed that will live. Here is the brief story.

The holder was being repaired, the gas had been removed, and air had been pumped into it instead of gas so that men could work inside, and the holder had risen about fifty feet. Two men were working inside the holder, one a foreman, and the other a labourer named Case, the latter in a diver's helmet. They were standing on a plank floating on the water. Fresh air was being pumped down to Case, who, so long as he kept on the helmet, was perfectly safe.

F. J. Cross

All at once the foreman found he was beginning to feel faint, so he told the labourer they would go up to the top for fresh air. But he had not the strength to carry out his purpose. The raft was pulled to the ladder by which they were to get out; but he was unable to ascend, and fell down in a fainting condition.

Then the labourer, regardless of the danger he was running, unscrewed his helmet, into which fresh air was being pumped, and, placing it quite near his fallen comrade, enabled him to get some of the air. The foreman tried in vain to get Case to put on the helmet; and his own strength was too slight to force him to do so. Indeed, he was in such a state of weakness that he fell on the raft, and knew no more till he once again found himself in a place of safety.

Now let us see how the foreman's rescue was effected, and at what cost. The men at the top of the holder had by this time become aware that something was wrong below; and two men, Chew and Smith by name, at once volunteered to go down below. They reached the plank, got a rope round the foreman's body, when they too began to feel the effects of the gas, and ascended the ladder, whilst the foreman was being hoisted up by means of the rope. Smith reached the top in a fainting condition. Chew never arrived there at all; for just as he got within a few feet of safety he became insensible, and fell down into the water below and was drowned. Meantime, Case had become jammed in between the plank and one of the stays; and so, when at length they removed him, life had passed away.

Such deeds are so often done by our working men that they think nothing about it. They do not know that they are heroes - that's the best of it! It is a fact to be thankful for that everywhere throughout the land, beneath the rough jackets of our artisans and labourers, beat hearts as true and fearless as those which have stormed the fort or braved the dangers of the battlefield.

F. J. Cross

THE COMMANDER OF THE "THIN RED LINE".

THE STORY OF SIR COLIN CAMPBELL.

It was the 21st Of October, 1808. Colin Campbell, not yet sixteen, had joined the army as ensign; and the battle of Vimiera was about to begin.

It was his "baptism of fire". Colin was in the rear company. His captain came for him, and taking the lad's hand walked with him up and down in front of the leading company for several minutes, whilst the enemy's guns were commencing to fire. Then he told the youngster to go back to his place.

"It was the greatest kindness that could have been shown to me at such a time; and through life I have felt grateful for it," wrote Colin Campbell in later life of this incident.

Soon after, the regiment to which he belonged formed part of the army that retreated to Corunna, when our troops suffered such terrible hardships. Colin Campbell had a rough time of it then. The soles of his boots were worn to pieces, and so long a time did he wear them without a change that the uppers stuck firmly to his legs; and, though the boots were soaked in hot water, the skin came away when they were taken off.

After the battle of Corunna, - when the British brought to bay, turned and defeated their foes, - it was Colin's regiment that had the honour of digging the grave in which their heroic commander Sir John Moore was buried.

Battle after battle followed ere the French troops were driven out of Spain, and Colin Campbell, young as he was, fought like a veteran.

At Barossa his bravery brought him into special notice, and at the San Sebastian he led a storming party, and was twice wounded in doing so.

First of all he was shot through the right thigh; but though a storm of bullets was flying about, and men falling thick around him, he was up again, and pressed onward only to be again shot down.

For his gallant conduct on this occasion he was specially mentioned in the despatch that the general commanding the forces sent to the Duke of Wellington.

A few weeks later the troops moved on, and fought at the battle of Bidassoa, Colin Campbell being left in the hospital to recover from his wounds.

But so little was it to his liking to stay in the rear that he escaped from the hospital, and managed not only to fight at Bidassoa, but to get wounded again!

He was, of course, reproved by his colonel; but who could be seriously angry with a youngster for such conduct? So when he was sent back to England to get healed of his wounds, he was made a captain at the early age of twenty-one.

Among the first things that Colin Campbell did when he received his captain's pay was to make his father an allowance of £30 or £40 a year; and later on it was an immense satisfaction for him to be able to provide both for his father and sister.

In the Chinese war of 1842 he was in command of the 98th Regiment. The tremendous heat of the country during the summer terribly thinned the ranks of his forces, and he lost over 400 men in eighteen months. He himself was struck down by sunstroke and fever; but, owing probably to his temperate and careful habits, he soon recovered.

After the Chinese war, Colin Campbell was busy in India, and at Chillianwallah was wounded in the arm. It was in this battle he narrowly escaped with his life. The day after the fight, when he was being assisted to take off his uniform, he found that a small pistol which had been put in his pocket without his knowledge was broken, his watch smashed, and his side bruised. A bullet had struck him, unperceived in the heat of the battle, and his life saved by its force having been arrested by the handle of the pistol.

In 1849 Colin Campbell was made a K.C.B. (Knight Commander of the Bath); so we must henceforth speak of him as "Sir" Colin.

March, 1853, saw Sir Colin Campbell in England; but though he had passed his sixtieth year, most of which had been spent in his country's service, his rest was not of long duration, as in 1854 he went out to the Crimea in command of the Highland brigade, consisting of the

42nd, 79th, and 93rd regiments. Sir Colin was proud of the splendid troops he commanded, and at the battle of the Alma they covered themselves with glory.

The 42nd (the Black Watch) were the first of the three regiments across the river Alma. Whilst ascending the height on the Russian side of the river, Sir Colin's horse was twice wounded, the second shot killing it; but he was soon mounted on another horse, leading his men to victory.

The Guards and Highlanders strove in friendly emulation who should be first in the Russian redoubt; but Sir Colin, well ahead of his own men was first in the battery shouting: -

"We'll hae nane but Highland bonnets here!" and his troops rushed in after him like lions.

The terrific charge of these fierce Highlanders, combined with their dress, struck terror into the hearts of the Russians; who said that they thought they had come to fight men, but did not bargain for demons in petticoats!

"Now, men," Sir Colin had said before the engagement, "you are going into battle. Remember this: Whoever is wounded - I don't care what his rank is - must lie where he falls till the bandsmen come to attend to him.... Be steady. Keep silent. Fire low. Now, men, the army will watch us. Make me proud of the Highland brigade!"

At the conclusion of that well-fought day the commander-in-chief, Lord Raglan, sent for Sir Colin. His eyes were full, his lips quivered, and he was

F. J. Cross

unable to speak; but he gave Campbell a hearty handshake and a look which spoke volumes.

That was a joyful day for Sir Colin.

"My men behaved nobly," he writes. "I never saw troops march to battle with greater *sang froid* and order than these three Highland regiments."

The Alma had been fought on 20th September, 1854, and on the 25th October was fought the battle of Balaclava, memorable for the "Thin Red Line". It looked, at one time, as if the heavy masses of Russian cavalry must entirely crush Sir Colin's Highlanders; and their commander, riding down the line of his troops, said: "Remember, there is no retreat from here, men; you must die where you stand".

"Ay, ay, Sir Colin, we'll do that," came the ready response. Now, it was usual, in preparing to receive a cavalry charge, for soldiers to be formed in a hollow square; but on this occasion Sir Colin ranged his men, two deep, in a *thin red line*, which has become memorable in the annals of the British army. The Russian cavalry were advancing, but, instead of the masses which were expected to make the attack, only about 400 came on.

Sir Colin's men, fierce and eager for the onset, would have dashed from behind the hillock where they were stationed, but for the stern voice commanding them to stand firm in their ranks.

The Russians hardly waited for their fire. Startled by the red-coated Britishers rising up at the word of their leader, they broke and fled; and the men of the 93rd, who, but a little before, had made up their minds to die where they stood, saw as in a dream their enemies scattered and broken; and the cloud of horsemen which had threatened to engulf and annihilate them, make no effort to snatch the victory which seemed within their grasp.

Before the Crimean war was over, Sir Colin resigned his command, and returned to England, as a protest against an affront he had received.

Honoured by the Queen with a command to attend her at Windsor, he was asked by her Majesty to return to the Crimea; and the veteran assented at once, declaring he would serve under a corporal if she wished it.

The Russian war was soon concluded; and Sir Colin thought that at length he had finished soldiering. But it was not to be. In the summer of 1857 the Indian Mutiny broke out, and on 11th July he was asked how soon he could start for India. The old soldier of sixty-five replied that he could go the same evening; and on the very next day, Sunday, he was on his way to take command of the British army in India.

As the Mutiny is alluded to briefly in the story of Havelock, I will only state that Sir Colin's vigorous, cautious, skilful policy ere long brought this fearful rebellion to a close.

For his able conduct of the war he was warmly thanked by the Queen; and at its conclusion was raised to the peerage, under the title of Lord Clyde. Colin Campbell was an admirable soldier, firm in discipline, setting a good example, ever thoughtful for the comfort and well-being of his men, sharing in all the hardships and perils they passed through. It is, therefore, not surprising that his men loved him.

Not that he was by any means a perfect man. He had a temper - a very hasty and passionate temper too, and one that troubled him a good deal; but he was on the watch for that to see it did not get the better of him.

Here is an entry from his diary of 5th March, 1846, showing something of the character of the man. "Anniversary of Barossa. An old story thirty years ago. Thank God for all His goodness to me'! Although I have suffered much from ill health, and in many ways, I am still as active as any man in the regiment, and quite as able as the youngest to go through fatigue."

Let us just glance at the way this victor in a hundred fights regarded the approach of death.

He prepared for his end with a humility as worthy of example as his deeds in the army had been. "Mind this," he said to his old friend General Eyre, "I die at peace with all the world."

He frequently asked Mrs. Eyre to pray with him, and to read the Bible aloud.

"Oh! for the pure air of Heaven," he once exclaimed, "that I might be laid at rest and peace on the lap of the Almighty!"

He suffered a good deal in his last illness, and at times would jump up as if he heard the bugle, and exclaim: -

"I am ready!"

And so; when he passed away on the 14th August, 1863, in his seventy-first year, "lamented by the Queen, the army, and the people," he was quite ready to meet that last enemy, death, whom he had faced so often on the field of battle.

F. J. Cross

A SAILOR BOLD AND TRUE.

STORIES OF LORD COCHRANE.

All who, forgetful of self, have striven to render their country free and glorious are true heroes. Of those who have been ready to lay down their lives for the welfare of Great Britain the number is legion. From them let us select one as a type of thousands of brave men who have helped to make Britain mistress of the ocean.

Thomas Cochrane, son of Lord Dundonald, took to the sea as a duck takes to the water. When he first went on board ship the lieutenant cared neither that he was Lord Cochrane nor that he was related to the captain of the ship. He did not spare him one jot; but made him do all kinds of work, just as if he had been plain Tom Smith. And so it came to pass that he got a thorough training, and, being a smart youth, was soon promoted.

Cochrane had the good fortune on one occasion to meet Lord Nelson, who in course of conversation said to him, "Never mind manoeuvres; always go at them".

This advice he certainly followed throughout his life; and he began pretty early too. For being in command of a sloop of 158 tons, called the *Speedy*, with fourteen small guns and fifty-one men, he happened to come across a good-sized Spanish vessel, with thirty-two big guns, and over 300 men. The Spaniard, of course, was going to seize on the little English ship, and, so to speak, gobble it up. But Cochrane, instead of waiting to be attacked, made for the Spaniard, and, after receiving the fire of all her guns, without delivering a shot, got right under the side of the *Gamo* (so the vessel was called), and battered into her with might and main. The Spaniards did not relish this, and were going to board the tiny English craft, but again they were forestalled; for Cochrane with all his men took the *Gamo* by storm, killed some, and frightened others; and ere long a marvellous sight was witnessed at Minorca, the great *Gamo* was brought by the *Speedy* into the harbour, with over 263 men on board, hale and hearty, whilst Cochrane never had a fifth of that number!

Ship after ship he took, till his name became a terror to the Spaniards and French; for he was so audacious, that no matter how big was the vessel he came across, nor how small his own, he "went at them," as Nelson had told him to do; and many a stately prize brought he home as the result of his daring and bravery.

One of the most gallant deeds he did was in connection with the defence of Rosas. Times had changed since the events related above, and Great Britain was now helping Spain in her struggle against France.

When he got to Rosas the place was within an ace of surrender. The French had pounded the defences into a deplorable condition.

Fort Trinidad, an important position, was about to be assaulted, the walls having been well-nigh beaten down by the fire of the enemy.

F. J. Cross

Cochrane however, with an immense quantity of sandbags, palisades, and barrels, made it pretty secure. But he did a cleverer thing even than this. There was a piece of steep rock, up which the besiegers would have to climb. This he covered with grease, so as to make it difficult to get a foothold, and planks with barbed hooks were placed ready to catch those who were rash enough to seek their aid.

The assault was delivered - up the rock came the French, and - down they tumbled in dozens and hundreds. Those who caught hold of the planks were hooked; and, to crown all, a heavy fire was poured into them by the British.

During the siege the Spanish flag was shot away whilst a heavy cannonade was going on; but Cochrane, though the bullets were whistling about in every direction, calmly stepped down into the ditch, and rescued the flag.

When he was not fighting his country's battles at sea, he was besieging Parliament to bring about reforms in the Navy. This naturally brought him a good many enemies amongst rich and powerful people, who were making plenty of money out of the Government, and doing nothing for it. So, when these persons had a chance of bringing a charge of conspiracy against him, they were right glad of the opportunity; and in the end Cochrane was sent to prison.

Some there were who believed in his honour and uprightness. His wife was in all his trials a very tower of strength to him. The electors of Westminster, who had sent him to Parliament, never ceased to have faith in his truth and honour, and re-elected him when still in prison. Yet, for all this, it was between forty and fifty years before his innocence was completely proved!

In 1847, however, he was restored to his honours by her Majesty the Queen; and in 1854 he was made a Rear Admiral of England.

F. J. Cross

A ROUGH DIAMOND THAT WAS POLISHED.

THE STORY OF JOHN CASSELL.

"I were summat ruff afore I went to Lunnon," said John Cassell.

He had called to see his friend Thomas Whittaker, who was staying at Nottingham, and John was announced as "the Manchester carpenter".

He was dressed on the occasion in a suit of clothes which a Quaker friend had given him; but Cassell being tall and thin, and the Quaker short and stout, they did not altogether fit!

The trousers were too short, and the hat too big; accordingly, John's legs came a long way through the trousers, and his head went a good way in at the top. "It was something like taking a tin saucepan with the bottom out and using it as a scabbard for a broad sword," remarked one who knew him. He had on an old overcoat, and a basket of tools was thrown over his shoulder with which to earn his food in case temperance lecturing failed.

When John remarked that he was "summat ruff," the gentleman at whose house Mr. Whittaker was staying nearly had a fit; and after he had at length recovered his gravity he ejaculated, "Well, I would have given a guinea to have seen you before you did go".

Yet John Cassell was a diamond - though at that time the roughest specimen one could come across from the pit's mouth to the Isle of Dogs. His ideas were clear cut; he had confidence in himself, he meant to make a name in the world, - and he *did*.

John Cassell was born in Manchester in 1817. His father, the bread-winner of the family, had the misfortune to meet with an injury which entirely disabled him, and from the effects of which he died when John was quite young. His mother worked hard for her own and her son's support, and had little time left to look very particularly to the education of her boy. He, however, grew up strong and hardy.

It is true that when he ought to have been at school he was often at play, or seeing something of the world, its sights and festivities, on his own account. True, also, that he tumbled into the river, and nearly ended his career at a very early age. Still he survived his river catastrophe; and, though he gained little book learning, possessed such a good and retentive memory, and was so observant, that his mind became stored with vivid impressions of the scenes and surroundings of his youth, which he related with great effect in after-life.

He had, of course, to begin work at an early age. First of all, he went into a cotton factory, and later to a velveteen factory; then, having a taste for carpentering, he took to it as a trade, though he was at best but a rough unskilled workman, tramping about the country, and doing odd jobs wherever he could get them.

F. J. Cross

One day John Cassell was working at the Manchester Exchange when he was persuaded to go and hear Dr. Grindrod lecture on temperance. The lecture seems to have bitten itself into John's mind; for a little later on, in July, 1835, after hearing Mr. Swindlehurst lecture, he signed the pledge. That was the unsuspected turning-point of carpenter John's life.

After this he attended meetings and took an active part on the platform, and became known as "the boy lecturer". Though he was dressed in fustian, and wore a workman's apron, he spoke effectively, and his words went to the hearts of his hearers. His originality of style, too, pleased the audiences of working people whom he addressed.

In 1836 John Cassell made his first move towards London.

He worked his way to town, and lectured on the road. He carried a bell, and with that brought together his audiences.

At times he was very roughly handled by the crowd; yet this had no effect upon him, except to make him the more determined.

His clothes became threadbare, his boots worn out, his general appearance dilapidated; but he got help from a few good people, who saw the hero beneath his rags.

He was three weeks accomplishing the journey; and when he arrived in London spent the first day in search of work, which he failed to obtain.

In the evening, seeing that a temperance meeting was

to be held in a hall off the Westminster Road, he went to it; and asked to be allowed to speak. Some of those on the platform viewed with distrust the gaunt, shabby, travel-stained applicant. But he would take no denial, and soon won cheers from the audience. When he stopped short, after a brief address, someone shouted "Go on". "How can a chap go on when he has nothing to say?" came the ready reply. That night he had no money in his pocket to pay for a bed; so he walked the streets of London through the weary hours till dawn of day.

Other temperance meetings he addressed; for his heart and mind were full of that subject. After one of the meetings a gentleman questioned him as to his means; and, finding the straits he was in, asked if he were not disheartened.

"No," replied John; "it is true I carry all my wealth in my little wallet, and have only a few pence in my pocket; but I have faith in God I shall yet succeed."

Struck by his manifest sincerity, the gentleman introduced him next day to a friend who took a warm interest in the temperance cause.

"Which wouldst thou prefer, carpentering or trying to persuade thy fellow-men to give up drinking, and to become teetotalers?" he asked.

Without hesitation John Cassell replied: -

"The work of teetotalism."

"Then thou shalt have an opportunity, and I will stand thy friend."

F. J. Cross

John Cassell now went forth as a disciple of the temperance cause. Remembering his experiences on the way to London he furnished himself with a watchman's rattle, with which he used to call together the people of the villages he visited.

A temperance paper thus speaks of him in 1837: -

"John Cassell, the Manchester carpenter, has been labouring, amidst many privations, with great success in the county of Norfolk. He is passing through Essex - (where he addressed the people, among other places, from the steps leading up to the pulpit of the Baptist chapel, with his carpenter's apron twisted round his waist) - on his way to London. He carries his watchman's rattle - an excellent accompaniment of temperance labour."

Cassell had a great regard for Thomas Whittaker. It was an address given by this gentleman which had first made him wish to become a public man.

When he called on Mr. Whittaker in Nottingham, as already related, after some conversation had taken place, he remarked: -

"I should like to hear thee again, Tom".

"Well," remarked Whittaker as a joke, "you can if you go with me to Derby."

John accepted the invitation forthwith, much to his friend's chagrin, who was bothered to know what to do with him; for he was under the impression that some members of the family where he expected to lodge would not give a very hearty welcome to this rough fellow.

This is Mr. Whittaker's narrative of the sequel: -

"We walked together to Derby that day. At the meeting he spoke a little, and pleased the people. When the meeting was over, he said: -

"'Can't I sleep with you?'

"'Well,' I said, 'I have no objection; but, you know, *I* am only a lodger.'

"However, go with me he *would*, and *did*. That was the man. When John made up his mind to do a thing he did it; and to that feature in his character, no doubt, much of his future success may be attributed. The gentleman at whose house he met me at Nottingham, and who was ashamed of him, subsequently became his servant, and touched his hat to him; and John has pulled up at my own door in his carriage, with a liveried servant, when I lived near to him in London."

John Cassell was now in the thick of the fight. In those days the opposition to the Gospel of Temperance was keen and bitter. Sometimes there were great disturbances at the meetings, sometimes he was pelted with rubbish, at times he did not know where to turn for a night's lodging. It was, on the whole, a fierce conflict; but John was nothing daunted.

It is, of course, impossible to sum up the amount of a man's influence. John Cassell scattered the seed of temperance liberally. Here is a case showing how one of the grains took root, and grew up to bear important fruit.

F. J. Cross

The Rev. Charles Garrett, the celebrated teetotal President of the Wesleyan Conference, writing several years after John Cassell's death, says: -

"I signed the pledge of total abstinence in 1840, after hearing a lecture on the subject by the late John Cassell. I have therefore tried it for more than thirty years. It has been a blessing to me, and has made me a blessing to others."

How to cure the curse of drink, what to give in its place when the pleasures of the glass were taken away - that was the problem which many have tried to solve. None more successfully than John Cassell.

At a meeting in Exeter Hall he suddenly put a new view before his audience. "I have it!" he exclaimed.

"The remedy is education. Educate the working men and women, and you have a remedy for the crying evil of the country. Give the people mental food, and they will not thirst after the abominable drink which is poisoning them."

He had hitherto been doing something to assist the temperance cause by the sale of tea and coffee, and he now turned his attention to the issue of publications calculated to benefit the cause.

Having, at the age of twenty-four, married Mary Abbott, he became possessed of additional means for carrying out his publishing schemes.

Cheap illustrated periodicals began to issue from the press under his superintendence, and copies were multiplied by the hundred thousand.

He never forgot that he had been a working man, and one of the first publications he started was called *The Working Man's Friend*.

It is not necessary to say more. Though John Cassell died comparatively young - he was only forty-eight when his death took place in 1865 - he had done a grand life's work; and the soundness of his judgment is shown by the fact that works which he planned retain their hold upon the people to this day.

John Cassell had his ambitions, but they were of a very simple kind.

"I started in life with one ambition," he said, "and that was to have a clean shirt every day of my life; this I have accomplished now for some years; but I have a second ambition, and that is to be an MAP., and represent the people's cause; then I shall be public property, and you may do what you like with me." This latter desire he would doubtless have realised but for his early decease.

F. J. Cross

"A BRAVE, FEARLESS SORT OF LASS."

THE STORY OF GRACE DARLING.

She was not much of a scholar, she could not spell as well as a girl in the third standard, she lived a quiet life quite out of the busy world; and yet Grace Darling's name is now a household word.

Let us see how that has come about.

William Darling, Grace's father, was keeper of the Longstone Lighthouse on the Farne Islands, off the coast of Northumberland. Longstone is a desolate rock, swept by the northern gales; and woe betide the ship driven on its pitiless shores!

Mr. Darling and his family had saved the lives of many persons who had been shipwrecked ere that memorable day of which I will tell you.

On the night of the 5th September, 1838, the steamer *Forfarshire*, bound from Hull to Dundee, was caught in a terrific storm off the Farne Islands. Her machinery became damaged and all but useless, and the vessel drifted till the sound of the breakers told sixty-three persons composing the passengers and crew that death was near at hand.

The captain made every effort to run the ship in between the Islands and the mainland, but in vain; and about three o'clock on the morning of the 6th September the vessel struck on the rock with a sickening crash.

A boat was lowered, into which nine of the passengers got safely, whilst others lost their lives in attempting to do so. These nine were saved during the day by a passing vessel.

The *Forfarshire* meantime was the sport of the waves, which threatened every minute to smash her in pieces.

Before long, indeed, one wave mightier than the rest lifted her bodily on to the sharp rocks and broke her in two. Her after-part was swept away, and the captain, his wife, and those who were in that portion of the vessel, were drowned. The fore-part meantime remained fast on the rocks, lashed by the furious billows.

That morning Grace was awakened by the sound of voices in distress, and dressing quickly she sought her father.

They listened, and soon their worst fears were confirmed. Near at hand, but still quite beyond reach of help, could be heard the despairing shrieks of the shipwrecked crew.

To attempt to rescue them seemed quite out of the question. That was apparent at once to William Darling, skilful boatman though he was, and brave as a lion.

The sea was so terrific that it was ten chances to one against a boat being able to keep afloat.

But Grace entreated: "Father, we must not let them perish. I will go with you in the boat, and God will give us success."

In vain Mrs. Darling urged that the attempt was too perilous to be justified, and reproached Grace for endeavouring to persuade her father to run such unwarrantable risks.

William Darling saw plainly how many were the chances against success. Even if the boat was not at once swamped, two persons alone, and one of them only a girl, were insufficient for the work; for, supposing they reached the wreck, they would probably be too exhausted to get back.

No, duty did not demand such an act; and for a time he declined to put out.

But Grace was quite firm. This girl of three and twenty, never very robust, had marvellous strength of will; and, her mind being set on attempting the rescue, she prevailed over both her father's judgment and her mother's entreaties; and into that awful sea the boat was at length launched. Though every billow threatened to engulf the frail craft, yet it nevertheless rode through the mountainous waves and drew near the rock where the helpless men and women were standing face to face with death. When it was sufficiently close to the shore William Darling sprang out to help the weary perishing creatures, whilst Grace was left to manage the boat unaided.

It was now that her courage was put to the severest test. At this critical moment the lives of her father and all the survivors depended upon her judgment and skill.

Well did her past experience and cool nerve then serve her. Alone and unaided she kept the boat in a favourable position in the teeth of that pitiless gale; and as soon as her father signalled to her she waited for an opportune moment and rowed in. Ere long, in spite of the fury of wind and wave, they had got all aboard, and rowed back in safety to the lighthouse.

The passengers who were rescued told the story of Grace's courage; and soon the tale was in every newspaper.

George Darling, Grace's brother, speaking of this deed fifty years after, says: "She always considered, as indeed we all did, that far too much was made of what she did. She only did what was her duty in the circumstances, brought up among boats, so to speak, and used to the sea as she was. Still she was always a brave, fearless sort of lass, and very religious too - there's no doubting that. But it was never her wish that people should make so much of what she did."

A great deal was made of the deed certainly, but surely not too much. A subscription was set on foot, and £700 presented to her, besides innumerable presents.

Four years later Grace died, much lamented by all who knew her.

Doubtless many a time, before and since, faith as strong, and bravery as heroic, have been shown, and have passed unrecorded and unnoticed by men. But duty performed in simple faith and without expectation of reward brings inward peace and joy greater than any outward recognition can give.

* * * * *

GRACE DARLING THE SECOND.

Whilst these pages were passing through the press the news came of the bravery of another Grace Darling in a far-off land.[1]

[Footnote 1: See letter of Rev. Ellis of Rangoon in *Times* of 25th May, 1894.]

Miss Darling was head mistress of the Diocesan School at Amherst near Rangoon, and her pupils were bathing in the sea when one of them was bitten in the leg by a shark or alligator. Alarmed by this terrible shock she lost her balance and was being carried away by the tide when her sister and the head mistress both went to the rescue. Miss Grace Darling had succeeded in getting hold of her when she too was bitten and disappeared under the water. The sister behind cried out for help, at the same time seizing the head mistress and vainly endeavouring to keep her head above water. In the end some native sailors came to the rescue and dragged all three out, but Grace Darling and the favourite pupil whom she had endeavoured to save were both dead.

A FRIEND OF LEPERS.

THE STORY OF FATHER DAMIEN.

Of all forms of disease leprosy is perhaps the most terrible. The lepers of whom we read in the Bible were obliged to dwell alone outside the camp; and even king Uzziah, when smitten with leprosy, mighty monarch though he was, had to give up his throne and dwell by himself to the end of his days.

In the far-off Sandwich (or Hawaiian) Islands in the Pacific Ocean there are many lepers; but the leprosy from which they suffer is of a more fatal kind than that which is spoken of in the Bible.

So as to prevent the spread of the disease, the lepers are sent to one of the smaller islands, where there is a leper village, in which those who are afflicted remain until their death.

When a shipload of these poor creatures leaves Honolulu for the little Isle of Molokai there is great wailing by the relatives of those sent away, for they know the parting is final.

The disease is not slow in running its course. After about four years it usually attacks some vital organ, and the leper dies.

F. J. Cross

Until the year 1873 the lot of the lepers on their help them, that all hearts were turned in love towards him.

He first made the discovery when he had been at Molokai about ten years. He happened to drop some boiling water on his foot, and it gave him no pain. Then he knew he had the leprosy.

Yet he was not cast down when he became aware of the fact, for he had anticipated it.

"People pity me and think me unfortunate," he remarked; "but I think myself the happiest of missionaries."

In 1889, sixteen years after landing at Molokai, Father Damien died.

When he was nearing his end, he wrote of the disease as a "providential agent to detach the heart from all earthly affection, prompting much the desire of a Christian soul to be united - the sooner the better - with Him who is her only life".

During his last illness he suffered at times intensely; yet was patient, brave, and full of thoughtfulness for his people through it all, and looked forward with firm hope to spending Easter with his Maker. He died on the 15th April, 1889. "A happier death," wrote the brother who nursed him in his illness, "I never saw."

There, far away amongst those for whom he gave his life, lie the remains of one of the world's great examples, whose name will ever be whispered with reverence, and who possessed to a wonderful extent "the peace which the world cannot give".

A GREAT ARCTIC EXPLORER.

THE STORY OF SIR JOHN FRANKLIN.

The passage to the North Pole is barred by ice fields and guarded by frost and snow more securely than Cerberus guarded the approach to the kingdom of Pluto.

For three centuries and more the brave and daring of all nations have tried to pass these barriers. Hundreds of men have been frozen to death, hundreds have died of starvation; and yet men continue to hazard their lives to find out this secret of Nature.

One of the bravest arctic explorers was Sir John Franklin, who, after many wonderful adventures, finally died with his companions amid the frozen seas of the north.

As a little boy, "life on the ocean wave" was to John Franklin a delightful day-dream. Once when at school he walked twelve miles to get a sight of the sea and a taste of the salt air; and such was his desire for a seafaring career that although his father was at first very much opposed to the idea, yet when he found how strongly Franklin had set his heart upon a sailor's life, he got him a place on a war-ship where John took part in the battle of Copenhagen.

F. J. Cross

Then he was shipwrecked on the coast of Australia, did some fighting in the Straits of Malacca, and was present at the great battle of Trafalgar.

After this he had his first taste of Arctic adventure, having received a commission from the Government to explore the Coppermine, one of the great rivers of Canada, which discharges its waters into the Arctic Ocean. Down this river sailed Franklin and his companions. They encountered rapids and falls, and all kinds of obstacles, and met with many dangers and disasters.

The first winter they were nearly starved to death. They stayed at Fort Enterprise; but, long before the spring returned, they found their food was all but finished, and the nearest place to get more was five hundred miles away, over a trackless desert of snow. One of their number, however, tramped the whole weary way, and brought back food to his starving leader and companions.

Next summer, Franklin descended the river to its mouth, and embarking in canoes he and his followers made towards Behring Strait, from which they were ere long driven back by their old dread enemy - starvation. For many days on their return journey they had nothing to live upon but rock moss, which barely kept them alive. They became so worn and ill that they could only cover a few miles a day, and Franklin fainted from exhaustion.

For eight days they waited on the banks of a river which it was necessary to pass, but which they had no means of crossing. One of the men tried to swim across and was nearly drowned, and despair seized on the party, for they thought the end had come. But there was one man among them who could not believe God would leave them to perish, and spurred on by this thought he gathered rock moss in sufficient quantities to preserve their lives; and, hope springing up again, they made a light raft on which they passed over to the other side.

Then Franklin set off with eight men to get assistance, whilst others remained to care for the sick. He and three companions only arrived at Fort Enterprise. They had to endure a fearful journey, during which they ate their very boots to preserve life. To their bitter disappointment when they got there they found the place deserted! Then they attempted to go to the next settlement; but Franklin utterly broke down on the way, and was with difficulty got back to Fort Enterprise. Here they were joined by two of the party who had been left behind, the others having perished on the way.

The night of their reunion, the six survivors had a grand feast. A partridge had been shot, and for the first time during an entire month these men tasted flesh food. Later on, sitting round the fire they had kindled, words of hope and comfort were read from the Bible, and the men joined heartily together in prayer and thanksgiving. Shortly after, friendly Indians arrived with supplies of food, and Franklin with the survivors of his party returned safely to England.

After this, Franklin made other expeditions, gaining fame and honour by his explorations, and was for seven years Lieutenant-Governor of Tasmania.

Then in 1845, when he was in his sixtieth year, he

went out in the service of the Admiralty to attempt the passage through the Arctic Ocean. Leaving England in May, 1845, in command of the *Erebus* and *Terror*, with a body of the most staunch and experienced seamen, he sailed into the Arctic Seas. They were last seen by a whaler on the 26th of July that year, and then for years no word of their fate reached Great Britain.

Not that England waited all this time before she sent to discover what had befallen them. The Government was stirred into action by the pleadings of Lady Franklin. Expedition after expedition left our shores. America and France joined in the search. Five years later was discovered the place in which the *Erebus* and *Terror* had first wintered; but it was left for Dr. John Rae to find out from the Esquimaux in 1854 that the ships had been crushed in the ice, and that Franklin and his companions had died of fatigue and starvation.

The final relics of the Franklin Expedition were discovered by McClintock and a party of volunteers. Starting from England in a little vessel called *The Fox* he and his crew passed through a hundred dangers from shipwreck, icebergs, and other perils. But at length, in April, 1858, they found on King William's Island the record which told plainly and fully the fate of Franklin and his companions.

The document contained two statements, one written in 1846, mentioning that Sir John Franklin and all were well; and a second, written in 1848, to say that they had been obliged to abandon the *Erebus* and *Terror*, that Sir John Franklin had died in June, 1847, and that they had already lost nine officers and fifteen men.

Other traces of the sad end which overtook the

expedition were also found. In a boat were discovered two skeletons; and amongst other books a Bible, numerous passages in which were underlined, showing that these gallant men in their last hours had the comfort of God's Word to support them when earthly hopes had passed away.

The object for which Sir John Franklin had sailed, viz., the discovery of the North West passage, had been attained, but no single man of the expedition, alas, lived to enjoy the fruits of the discovery.

F. J. Cross

A SAVIOUR OF SIX

THE STORY OF FIREMAN FORD.

In the waiting room at the head quarters of the London Fire Brigade, in Southwark Street, London, is an oak board on which are fixed a number of brass tablets, bearing the names of men who are entitled to a place on this "Roll of Honour".

From amongst these let us take one, and tell briefly what befell him. It will serve as a sample of the dangers which beset the fireman daily in the pursuit of his duty.

"Joseph Andrew Ford," so runs the official record, "lost his life at a fire which occurred at 98 Gray's Inn Road, at about 2 a.m. on the 7th of October, 1871.

"Ford was on duty with the fire escape stationed at Bedford Row, and he was called to the fire a few minutes before 2 a.m., and proceeded there with the utmost speed.

"Before he reached the fire, three persons had been rescued by the police, who took them down from the second-floor window by means of a builder's ladder; and, on his arrival, there were seven persons in the third floor, six in the left-hand window, and one in the right-hand window.

"He pitched his escape to the left-hand window, and with great difficulty and much exertion and skill succeeded in getting the six persons out safely (the woman in the right-hand window being in the meanwhile rescued by the next escape that arrived, in charge of fireman W. Attwood); and Ford was in the act of coming down himself when he became enveloped in flame and smoke, which burst out of the first-floor window; and, after some struggling in the wire netting, he fell to the pavement.

"Ford was evidently coming down the shoot when his axe handle or some of his accoutrements became entangled in the wire netting; so that, to clear himself, he had to break through, and, while struggling to do so, he got so severely burned that his recovery was hopeless.

"It was a work of no ordinary skill and difficulty to save so many persons in the few moments available for the purpose; and, when it is mentioned that some of them were very old and crippled, it is no exaggeration to say that it would be impossible to praise too highly Ford's conduct on this occasion, which has resulted so disastrously to himself.

"He was thirty-one years of age when he met his death, and he left a wife and two children to mourn his loss."

That's all the official record says - simple, calm, straightforward - like Joseph Ford's conduct on that night.

I suppose that next morning two pairs of bright little yes were on the watch for Joseph Ford; and perchance

F. J. Cross

four pattering feet ran to the door when the knock came; and that two little minds dimly realised that father had been called to a far-off country, where some day they would see him. And it may be that a brave woman, into whose life the sunlight had shined, was stricken with grief and bowed down. But all I know for certain is, that Joseph Ford died in the performance of his duty. He did a brave night's work. Six lives saved from the angry flames - old and crippled some of the terror-stricken folk were - and he took them down so carefully, so tenderly, and landed them all safely below.

His work was over. He had saved every life he could; and glad of heart, if weary of limb, he turned with a thankful mind to do just the simplest thing in the world - viz., to descend the escape he had been down so many times before.

He was young and strong; safety was only thirty feet or so below; and the people were waiting to welcome and cheer the victor.

Only thirty feet between him and safety! Yet the man was "fairly roasted" in the escape.

Men have been burnt at the stake and tortured, and limbs have been stretched on the rack, and people have been maimed by thumbscrews and bootscrews, and put inside iron figures with nails that tear and pierce. All this have they suffered in pursuit of duty, or at the bidding of conscience; and of such and of brave Joseph Ford there comes to us across the ages - a saying spoken long ago, to the effect that "he that loseth his life shall save it": and we need to remember that saying in such cases as that of Fireman Ford.

A BLIND HELPER OF THE BLIND.

THE STORY OF ELIZABETH GILBERT.

"A fine handsome child, with flashing black eyes!" Thus was Elizabeth Gilbert described at her birth in 1826; but at the age of three an attack of scarlet fever deprived her of eyesight; and thenceforth, for upwards of fifty years, the beautiful things in the world were seen by her no more.

Her parents were most anxious that she should take part in all that was going on in the household, in order that she should feel her misfortune as little as possible. So she lived in the midst of the family circle, sharing in their sports, their meals, and their entertainments, and being treated just as one of the others; yet with a special care and devotion by her father, Dr. Gilbert, whose heart went out in deep love towards his little sightless daughter.

Bessie was fond of romping games, and preferred by far getting a few knocks and bumps to being helped or guided by others when she was at play. She was by nature passionate, yet she gradually subdued this failing. She was a general favourite; and, when any petition had to be asked of father, it was always Bessie who was put forward to do it, as the children knew how good were her chances of being successful in her mission.

She was educated just like other girls, except that her lessons were read to her. She made great progress, and was a very apt pupil in French, German, and other subjects; but arithmetic she cordially disliked. Imagine for an instant the drudgery of working a long division sum with leaden type and raised, figures; think of all the difficulty of placing the figures, and the chances of doing the sum wrong; and then it will not cause surprise that the blind girl could never enjoy arithmetic, although in mental calculation she showed herself later on to be very clever.

When she was about ten years old, the Duchess of Kent and the Princess Victoria visited Oxford, where Bessie then lived with her parents. On her return home Bessie exclaimed: "Oh, mamma, I have *seen* the Duchess of Kent, and she had on a brown silk dress". Indeed, the child had such a vivid imagination that she saw mentally the scenes and people described to her.

And, so though no glimmer of light from the sun reached her, the child was not dull or unhappy. She listened to the birds with delight, and knew their songs; she loved flowers and liked people to describe them to her; and she was fond of making expeditions to the fields and meadows.

But as Bessie grew up she began to feel some of the sadness and loneliness natural to her lot. Her sisters could no longer be constantly with her as in the nursery days; and though she made no complaint, nor spoke of it to those around her, yet she felt it none the less keenly.

By this time her father had become Bishop of Chichester.

When Bessie was twenty-seven years old an idea was suggested which was the means of giving her an object in life, and affording her an opportunity of doing a great work for the blind.

It was her sister Mary who first spoke about it, having seen with sorrow how changed the once happy blind sister had become, and longing to lighten her burden.

Bessie listened to the facts which were set before her of the need that existed for some one to give a helping hand to the blind in London. She made many inquiries into the condition of the sightless, and then thought out a scheme for helping them.

Some of her friends considered it a great mistake for her to undertake such a mission. "Don't work yourself to death," said one of her acquaintances.

"Work to death!" she replied with a happy laugh. "I am working to life."

But if a few were opposed, her parents, brothers, sisters, and the majority of those she loved, were in hearty sympathy.

So in May, 1854, Bessie commenced her life work. Seven blind men were given employment at their own homes in London; materials were supplied to them at cost price, they manufactured them, and received the full price that the articles were sold for.

This, of course, entailed a loss; but Bessie had been

left a legacy by her godmother, which gave her an income of her own, and a large portion of this she continued to devote throughout her life to helping the blind.

A cellar was rented in New Turnstile Street, Holborn, at a charge of eighteenpence a week. A manager, named Levy, was engaged at a salary of half a crown a week and a commission on sales. He was a blind man himself, and a blind carpenter was engaged to assist in making the storehouse presentable.

It was a small beginning, certainly, but it was not long ere Levy's wages were largely increased, and trade began to grow in response to Miss Gilbert's efforts. From the cellar in Holborn a move was made to a better room, costing half a crown a week; and then, within little more than a year from the commencement, a house and shop were taken at a rent of £26 a year.

The increase in expenses as the scheme developed rendered it necessary to ask for public assistance. By the bishop's advice a committee was formed, and money collected.

By 1856, Miss Gilbert thought her work far enough advanced to bring it under the notice of Her Majesty, who, having asked for and received full particulars, sent a very kind letter of encouragement with a donation of £50.

This gracious acknowledgment of the work in which Miss Gilbert was engaged not only gave sincere pleasure to the blind lady herself, but helped on her scheme immensely. And the Queen did more than contribute money: orders for work were sent from

Windsor Castle, Osborne and Balmoral; and the blind people delighted in saying that they were making brooms for the Queen. The benefit to the blind was not confined to what Miss Gilbert was doing herself, but general interest in their welfare was excited in all parts of the kingdom.

Naturally, many difficulties had to be encountered. Blind people applied for work who wished for alms instead; and arrangements necessary for carrying out so large a scheme entailed a good deal of labour on Miss Gilbert's part. Yet she was very happy in her mission, which attracted numerous friends occupying positions of eminence.

Miss Gilbert herself gave £2000 to the Association as an endowment fund, and others contributed liberally too. One day a strange old lady came to see her, and left with her £500 in bank notes. She did not even give her name; and a further gift of £500 was received the same year from a gentleman who felt interested in the work.

Up to the close of her life, which ended in 1885, Elizabeth Gilbert continued to take an active interest in the affairs of the Association. Notwithstanding her own weak and failing health she laboured on, winning the love and gratitude of the blind, and accomplishing a great work of which any one might feel justly proud.

A GREAT TRAVELLER IN THE AIR.

SOME ANECDOTES OF JAMES GLAISHER.

For many years past men of science have been engaged in ascending far up amongst the clouds for the purpose of finding out as much as possible about the various currents of air, the electrical state of the atmosphere, the different kinds of clouds, sound, temperature and such matters.

One of the most eminent balloonists of modern times, Mr. James Glaisher, was many times in danger of losing his life whilst in pursuit of knowledge miles above the earth.

His first ascent was made from Wolverhampton on the 17th of July, 1862. It was very stormy at the time of starting. Before he and Mr. Coxwell got fairly off they very nearly came to grief; for the balloon did not rise properly, but dragged the car along near the ground, so that if they had come against any chimney or high building they would probably have been killed.

However, fortunately, they got clear and were soon high up above the clouds, with a beautiful blue sky, and the air so pleasantly warm that they needed no extra clothing, as is usually the case when in the upper region of the atmosphere. When they were about four miles high Mr. Glaisher found the beating of his heart become very distinct, his hands and lips turned to a dark bluish colour, and he could hardly read the instruments. Between four and five miles high he felt a kind of sea sickness.

Mr. Coxwell began to think they might be getting too near the Wash for safety, and they therefore came down quickly, and reached the earth with such force that the scientific instruments were nearly all broken. In their descent they passed through a cloud 8000 feet (or over a mile and a half) thick!

On the 5th of September, 1862, Mr. Glaisher and Mr. Coxwell made one of the most remarkable ascents in the history of ballooning. It nearly proved fatal to both.

Up to the time they reached the fifth mile Mr. Glaisher felt pretty well. What happened afterwards is best described by himself.

"When at the height of 26,000 feet I could not see the fine column of the mercury in the tube; then the fine divisions on the scale of the instrument became invisible. At that time I asked Mr. Coxwell to help me to read the instruments, as I experienced a difficulty in seeing them. In consequence of the rotary motion of the balloon, which had continued without ceasing since the earth was left, the valve line had become twisted, and he had to leave the car, and to mount into the ring above to adjust it. At that time I had no suspicion of other than temporary inconvenience in seeing. Shortly afterwards I laid my arm upon the table, possessed of its full vigour but directly after, being desirous of using it, I found it powerless. It must have lost its power momentarily. I then tried to move the other arm, but

F. J. Cross

found it powerless also. I next tried to shake myself, and succeeded in shaking my body. I seemed to have no legs. I could only shake my body. I then looked at the barometer, and whilst I was doing so my head fell on my left shoulder. I struggled, and shook my body again, but could not move my arms. I got my head upright, but for an instant only, when it fell on my right shoulder; and then I fell backwards, my back resting against the side of the car, and my head on its edge. In that position my eyes were directed towards Mr. Coxwell in the ring. When I shook my body I seemed to have full power over the muscles of the back, and considerable power over those of the neck, but none over my limbs....I dimly saw Mr. Coxwell in the ring, and endeavoured to speak, but could not do so; when in an instant black darkness came over me, and the optic nerve lost power suddenly. I was still conscious, with as active a brain as whilst writing this. I thought I had been seized with asphyxia, and that I should experience no more, as death would come unless we speedily descended. Other thoughts were actively entering my mind when I suddenly became unconscious, as though going to sleep. I could not tell anything about the sense of hearing; the perfect stillness of the regions six miles from the earth - and at that time we were between six and seven miles high - is such that no sound reaches the ear. My last observation was made at 29,000 feet.... Whilst powerless I heard the words 'temperature' and 'observation,' and I knew Mr. Coxwell was in the car, speaking to me, and endeavouring to rouse me; and therefore consciousness and hearing had returned. I then heard him speak more emphatically, but I could not speak or move. Then I heard him say, 'Do try; now do!' Then I saw the instruments dimly, next Mr. Coxwell, and very shortly I saw clearly. I rose in my seat and looked round, as though waking from sleep, and said to Mr. Coxwell, 'I have been insensible'. He said, 'Yes; and I too very nearly ...'. Mr. Coxwell informed me that he had lost the use of his hands, which were black, and I poured brandy over them."

When Mr. Coxwell saw that Mr. Glaisher was insensible he tried to go to him but could not, and he then felt insensibility coming over him. He became anxious to open the valve, but having lost the use of his hands he could not, and ultimately he did so by seizing the cord with his teeth and dipping his head two or three times.

During the journey they got to a height of 36,000 or 37,000 feet - about seven miles - that is to say, two miles higher than Mount Everest, the loftiest mountain in the world.

The year following Mr. Glaisher had a narrow escape from drowning.

He and Mr. Coxwell started from the Crystal Palace at a little past one o'clock on the 18th of April, 1863, and in an hour and thirteen minutes after starting were 24,000 feet high. Then they thought it would be just as well to see where they were, so they opened the valve to let out the gas, and came down a mile in three minutes. When, at a quarter to three, they were still 10,000 feet high Mr. Coxwell caught sight of Beachy Head and exclaimed: "What's that?" On looking over the car Mr. Glaisher found that they seemed to be overhanging the sea!

Not a moment was to be lost. They both clung on to the valve-line, rending the balloon in two places.

Down, down, down at a tremendous speed they went; the earth appeared to be coming up to them with awful swiftness; and a minute or two later with a resounding crash they struck the ground at Newhaven close to the sea. The balloon had been so damaged that it did not drag along, and though most of the instruments were smashed their lives were saved.

Much valuable scientific information has been obtained by Mr. Glaisher, and by those who, like him, have made perilous journeys into cloudland.

THE SOLDIER WITH THE MAGIC WAND.

THE STORY OF GENERAL GORDON.

"That great man and gallant soldier and true Christian, Charles Gordon." - THE PRINCE OF WALES.

Charles George Gordon was born at Woolwich on the 28th of January, 1833.

In early life he was delicate, and of all professions that of a soldier seemed least suitable for him. At school he made no mark in learning.

He was a fearless lad, with a strong will of his own. When he was only nine years old, and was yet unable to swim, he would throw himself into deep water, trusting to some older boy to get him out. He was threatened on one occasion that he should not go on a pleasure excursion because of some offence he had committed; and when afterwards he was given permission he stubbornly refused the treat - circus though it was, dear to the heart of a lad.

After passing through the Royal Military Academy at Woolwich he obtained in 1852 a commission as a Second Lieutenant of Engineers, and was sent out to the Crimea in December, 1854, with instructions to put up wooden huts for our soldiers, who were dying from cold in that icy land.

On his way he wrote from Marseilles to his mother; and, after telling her of the sights and scenes he has witnessed, mentions that he will leave Marseilles "D.V. on Monday for Constantinople".

Whilst in the Crimea he worked in the trenches twenty hours at a stretch times without number.

Once when he was leading a party at night he was fired at by his own sentries. On another occasion he was wounded in the forehead, and continued his work without showing any concern. He found it dull when no fighting was going on, but when there were bullets flying then it was exciting enough.

He was mentioned in the official despatches, and received from the French Government the Cross of the Legion of Honour.

Five years later Gordon was fighting with the English and French armies in China. Shortly after he was made commander of a force that was commissioned by the Emperor of China to put down a rebellion of the Taipings, of so dangerous a character that it threatened to overturn the monarchy.

Gordon had only about 3000 men, chiefly Chinese; and, notwithstanding the fact that when he took over the force it had just been demoralised by defeat, he soon proved himself more than a match for the rebel hordes. From one victory to another he led his men on, and cities fell in quick succession before him. His name ere long began to have the weight of an army in the mind of the rebels. Major Gordon, in fact, had made a great mark in the Chinese Empire.

On the 30th April Gordon was before the city of Taitsan, where three months before the same army which was now under his command had been defeated.

Three times his men rushed into the breach which the big guns had made. Twice they were hurled back; but for a third time Gordon urged them on, and their confidence in his leadership was such that they went readily; and this time, after a swift, sharp conflict, the city was won.

Europeans were fighting both with him and with the rebels. In the breach at Taitsan he came across two of the men he formerly had under his command. One was shot during the assault; the other cried out, "Mr. Gordon! Mr. Gordon! you will not let me be killed". "Take him down to the river and shoot him," said Gordon aloud. Aside he whispered, "Put him in my boat, let the doctor attend him, and send him down to Shanghai". He was stern and resolute enough where it was necessary, but underneath all was a heart full of love and pity.

During this war the only weapon Gordon carried was a cane; and men grew to regard this stick as a kind of magic wand, and Gordon as a man whom nothing could harm.

On one occasion when he was wounded he refused to retire till he was forcibly carried off the field by the doctor's orders.

After he had put an end to the rebellion the Emperor of China wanted to give him a large sum of money; but

F. J. Cross

Gordon, whose only object in fighting was to benefit the people, refused it, and left China as poor as he had entered it. He had various distinctions conferred upon him by the emperor, and the English people gave him the title of "Chinese Gordon".

A gold medal was presented to him by the emperor. Gordon, obliterating the inscription, sent it anonymously to the Coventry relief fund. Of this incident he wrote at a later period: "Never shall I forget what I got when I scored out the inscription on the gold medal. How I have been repaid a millionfold! There is now not one thing I value in the world. Its honours, they are false; its knicknacks, they are perishable and useless; whilst I live I value God's blessing - health; and if you have that, as far as this world goes, you are rich."

He returned to England and settled down at Gravesend, living quite simply, and working in his spare moments amongst the poor. To the boys he was a hero indeed. That was but natural, seeing he not only taught them to read and write, and tried to get them situations, but treated them as his friends.

In his sitting-room was a map of the world, with pins stuck in it marking the probable positions of the ships in which his "kings" (as he called his boys) were to be found in various parts of the world. Thus, as they moved from place to place, he followed them in his thoughts, and was able to point out their whereabouts to inquiring friends.

It is no wonder then that the urchins scrawled upon the walls of the town, "C.G. is a jolly good feller". "God bless the Kernel."

He visited the hospitals and workhouses, and all the money he received he expended on the poor; for he believed that having given his heart to God he had no right to keep anything for himself. He comforted the sick and dying, he taught in the Ragged and Sunday Schools. He lived on the plainest food himself, thus "enduring hardness". He even gave up his garden, turning it into a kind of allotment for the needy.

He had one object in life - to do good. His views were utterly unworldly and opposed to those generally held, but they were in the main right.

In 1874 Gordon went to Egypt, and at the request of the Khedive undertook the position of Governor-General of the Soudan, in the hope of being able to put down the slave trade.

He was beset with difficulties, and "worn to a shadow" by incessant work and ceaseless anxiety; but he would not give up.

In all his trials he felt the presence of God. As he watched his men hauling the boats up the rapids he "*prayed them up* as he used to do the troops when they wavered in the breaches in China".

Once his men failed in their attack on an offending tribe; and, believing they had been misled by the Sheik, wanted to punish him; but Gordon saw the other side of the man's character - "He was a brave patriotic man," he said; "and I shall let him go".

Here was his hope. "With terrific exertion," he writes, "in two or three years' time I may with God's administration make a good province - with a good army and a fair revenue and peace, and an increased trade, - also have suppressed slave raids." He felt it was a weary work before him, for he adds: "Then I will come home and go to bed, and never get up till noon every day, and never walk more than a mile". No wonder he was worn and tired, for he moved about the Soudan like a whirlwind. He travelled on camelback thousands of miles. In four months' time he had put down a dangerous rebellion that would have taken the Egyptians as many years - if, indeed, they could ever have done it at all.

This is the kind of way in which he won his victories. On one occasion with a few troops he arrived at a place called Dara. That great slave trader Suleiman, who had given Sir Samuel Baker so much trouble, was there at the head of 6000 men. Gordon rode into the place nearly alone, and told the commander to come and talk with him. Utterly taken aback the man did as he was requested, and afterwards promised obedience.

It is true he did not keep his promise; but after fighting several battles Suleiman was at length taken prisoner by Gordon's lieutenant; and so many were the crimes and cruelties that he had committed that he was condemned to death, and thus the slaves of Africa became rid of one of their worst oppressors.

The work begun by Baker was continued with great success by Gordon. He estimated that in nine months he liberated 2000 slaves. The suffering these poor creatures had gone through was appalling. Some of them when set free had been four or five days without water in the terrible heat of that hot country. Every caravan route showed signs of the horrible trade, by the bones of those who had fallen and died from exhaustion, unable to keep their ranks in the gang.

So great was the effect which the thought and sight of these sufferings produced on Gordon that he wrote in March, 1879: "I declare if I could stop this traffic I would willingly be shot this night".

Later on he was to give his life for these people; but the hour was not yet.

When Gordon was in Abyssinia King John took him prisoner. Brought before his Majesty, Gordon fairly took away the breath of the monarch by going up to him, placing his own chair beside the king's, and telling him that he would only talk to him as an equal.

"Do you know, Gordon Pasha," said the king, "that I could kill you on the spot if I liked?"

"I am perfectly aware of it," replied Gordon calmly; "so do it, if it is your royal pleasure."

"What! ready to be killed?" asked the king incredulously.

"Certainly. I am always ready to die," answered the pasha; "and so far from fearing your putting me to death you would confer a favour on me by so doing."

Upon this his Majesty gave up the idea of frightening him.

At the end of 1879 Gordon was free from the Soudan for the second time. In 1876 he had left it, as he thought, for good; but, as it turned out, it was only for a few weeks' holiday in England, and then back to quell the rebellion.

Even now it was destined that he should soon return once again and finally. But during the breathing time that now came to him, so far from leading an easy life or "never getting up till noon," he was in all parts of the world, from China to the Cape, from Ireland to India, still on the old mission of endeavouring to do a little good wherever he was.

Leopold II., King of the Belgians, who had a profound regard for Gordon, greatly desired that he should go out to the Congo; and in January, 1884, he was just preparing to start in his Majesty's service when on the 17th of that month a telegram from Lord Wolseley arrived, asking him to return to England.

At six o'clock next morning he was in London; and the same day, having received instructions from the Government, he was on his way for the last time to Khartoum.

The Egyptian garrisons of the Soudan towns were sore beset by the legions which were gathering beneath the banners of the Mahdi, who, flushed with victory, was threatening an eruption into Lower Egypt itself.

To extricate these garrisons without bloodshed if possible was Gordon's object. It was a forlorn hope; still if any one man could accomplish it Charles Gordon was that man.

But ere long it was found even beyond his powers; for after sending off a portion of the Khartoum population in safety down the river, the Mahdi's legions closed in upon him, and Khartoum was in a state of siege.

For nearly a year he held the city against all the forces of the enemy; and meantime Great Britain was stirred with a vehement desire to save the life of this devoted man.

In the autumn of 1884 a force under the command of Lord Wolseley was sent out to relieve Khartoum.

Whilst the British troops were slowly forcing their way up the river and across the desert, Khartoum was enduring a death agony.

By January, 1885, the city had been reduced to starvation. Donkeys, dogs, rats, everything indeed in the way of flesh, had been consumed; even boot leather, the straps of native bedsteads, and mimosa gum did not come amiss to the sorely-tried garrison.

Famine had produced lack of discipline on the part of some of the troops; and Gordon foresaw well what the end must be, though without a fear for himself.

You can read for yourself from the reproduction of the last page of his diary, written on the 14th December, 1884, his own estimate of the length of time he could hold out; and, though he managed to keep back the enemy for another month, yet on the 26th January, 1885, whilst yet Sir Charles Wilson and the British troops were fighting their way up the river Nile to his relief, Khartoum fell.

In the early dawn of that day the Mahdi assaulted the town in overwhelming force - whether helped by treachery is not exactly known; and before his well-fed, well-trained hosts, the feeble worn-out garrison gave way, the walls were scaled, the city taken, and the hero who had won the affection of many nations fell midst the people he had come to save.

It was on the whole a happy and fitting end. The mind cannot conceive Gordon rusting out; and the man lived so much in the presence of God that death was a welcome visitor.

"Like Lawrence," he wrote, "I have tried to do my duty"; and England confessed that right nobly he had done it.

Let those who wish to testify their love and veneration for this great man remember the Gordon Home for Boys at Chobham, which was founded to perpetuate his name. It is situated in the midst of Surrey; and here are to be found over two hundred boys rescued from the streets of our great cities.

The bracing life they lead in their country home soon brings the colour to their cheeks, and the training they receive fits them for becoming useful citizens and valuable servants of the State. Most of them join the army, and the Gordon boys are now to be found serving the Queen in every land.

"VALIANT AND TRUE."

THE STORY OF SIR RICHARD GRENVILLE.

One of the most glorious of the many battles of the British navy was fought on the 10th and 11th September, 1591, by Vice-Admiral Sir Richard Grenville, in his ship *The Revenge*, against a great fleet of Spanish vessels. The fight was described by the gallant Sir Walter Raleigh, from whose account (published in November, 1591) the facts given in the following narrative are taken.

If the story seems somewhat out of place amongst nineteenth century records, it is, nevertheless, such a unique display of stubborn heroism "under fire" that I have not hesitated to include it.

On the 10th of September, 1591 (31st August, old style), Lord Thomas Howard, with six of her Majesty's ships, five victualling ships, a barque and two or three pinnaces, was at anchor near Flores, one of the westerly islands of the Azores, when Captain Middleton brought the news that the Spanish fleet was approaching.

He had no sooner delivered his message than the Spaniards came in sight. The few ships at Lord Howard's command were in a very unready state for fighting. Many of the seamen were ill. Some of the ships' companies were procuring ballast, others getting in water.

Being so unprepared for the contest, and so greatly outnumbered, the British ships weighed their anchors and set sail. The last ship to get under weigh was *The Revenge*, as Sir Richard waited for the men left on the island, who would have otherwise been captured.

The master of the ship wanted him to "cut his mainsail and cast about, and to trust to the sailing of his ship"; but Sir Richard utterly refused to turn from the enemy, saying that he would rather choose to die than dishonour himself, his country, and her Majesty's ship, and informed his company that he would pass through the two squadrons in spite of them. He might possibly have been able to carry out his plan; but the huge *San Philip*, an immense vessel of 1500 tons, coming towards him as he was engaging other ships of the fleet, becalmed his sails and then boarded him. Whilst thus entangled with the *San Philip*, four other ships also boarded *The Revenge*.

"The fight thus beginning at three of the clocke in the after noone," says Sir Walter Raleigh, "continued verie terrible all that evening."

Before long, the *San Philip*, having received the fire of *The Revenge* at close quarters, "shifted herself with all diligence, utterly misliking her first entertainment".

The Spanish ships had a great number of soldiers on board, in some cases two hundred, in others five, and in some even eight hundred; whilst on *The Revenge* there were in all only one hundred and ninety persons, of whom ninety were sick.

After discharging their guns the Spanish ships endeavoured to board *The Revenge*; but, notwithstanding the multitude of their armed men, they were repulsed again and again, and driven back either into their ships or into the sea.

After the battle had lasted well into the night many of the British were slain or wounded, whilst two Spanish ships had been sunk. An hour before midnight Sir Richard Grenville was shot in the body, and a little later was wounded in the head, whilst the doctor who was attending him was killed.

The company on board *The Revenge* was gradually getting less and less; the Spanish ships, meanwhile, as they received a sufficient evidence of *The Revenge's* powers of destruction, dropped off, and their places were taken by others; and thus it happened that ere the morning fifteen ships had been engaged, and all were so little pleased with the entertainment provided that they were far more willing to listen to proposals for an honourable arrangement than to make any more assaults.

As Lord Tennyson writes: -

And the sun went down, and the stars came out far over the summer sea,
But never a moment ceased the fight of the one and the fifty-three.
Ship after ship the whole night long their high-built galleons came,

Ship after ship, the whole night long, with her
battle-thunder and flame;
Ship after ship, the whole night long, drew back
with her dead and her shame.
For some were sunk and many were shatter'd, and
so could fight us no more -
God of battles, was ever a battle like this in the
world before?

The Revenge had by this time spent her last barrel of
gunpowder; all her pikes were broken, forty of her best
men slain, and most of the remainder wounded. For her
brave defenders there was now no hope, - no powder,
no weapons, the masts all beaten overboard, all her
tackle cut asunder, her decks battered, nothing left
overhead for flight or below for defence.

Sir Richard, finding himself in this condition after
fifteen hours' hard fighting, and having received about
eight hundred shots from great guns, besides various
assaults from the enemy, and seeing, moreover, no way
by which he might prevent his ship falling into the
hands of the Spanish, commanded the master gunner,
whom he knew was a most resolute man, to split and
sink the ship. He did this that thereby nothing might
remain of glory or victory to the Spaniards: seeing that
in so many hours' fight, and with so great a navy, they
were not able to take her, though they had fifteen hours
in which to do so; and moreover had 15,000 men and
fifty-three ships of war against his single vessel of five
hundred tons.

He endeavoured to persuade his men to yield
themselves to God, and to the mercy of none else; that,
as they had repulsed so many enemies, they should not
shorten the honour of their nation by prolonging their

lives by a few hours or days.

The captain and master could not, however, see the matter in this light, and besought Sir Richard to have a care of them, declaring that the Spaniards would be ready to treat with them; and that, as there were a number of gallant men yet living whose wounds were not mortal, they might do their country and prince acceptable service hereafter. They also pointed out that as *The Revenge* had six feet of water in the hold and three shots under water, but weakly stopped, she must needs sink in the first heavy sea; which indeed happened a few days later. But Sir Richard refused to be guided by such counsels.

Whilst, however, the dispute was going on, the master of *The Revenge* opened communication with the Spaniards and concluded an arrangement fully honourable to the British, by which it was agreed that those on board *The Revenge* should be sent to England in due course; those of the better sort to pay a reasonable ransom, and meantime no one was to be imprisoned. The commander of the Spanish fleet agreed to this readily, not only because (knowing the disposition of his adversary) he feared further loss to his own side by prolonging the fight, but because he greatly admired the valour of Sir Richard Grenville, and desired to save his life. The master gunner, finding Sir Richard and himself alone in their way of thinking, would have slain himself rather than fall into the hands of the enemy, but was forcibly prevented from carrying out his intention and locked in his cabin.

Being sent for by Don Alfonso Bassan, the Spanish commander, Sir Richard made no objection to going, answering that he might do as he pleased with his body, for he esteemed it not. As he was being carried out of the ship he swooned, and reviving again desired the company to pray for him.

Though the Spaniards treated Sir Richard with every care and consideration, he died the second or third day after the fight, deeply lamented both by, the enemy and by his own men.

"Here die I, Richard Grenville," said he, "with a joyful and quiet mind; for that I have ended my life as a true soldier ought to do, that hath fought for his country, queen, religion and honour. Whereby my soul most joyfully departeth out of this body, and shall always leave behind it an everlasting fame of a valiant and true soldier, that hath done his duty as he was bound to do."

The reason the other British ships did not take part in the contest was that it was altogether hopeless; and that, had the admiral ordered it, the entire fleet would probably have fallen into the hands of the Spaniards, seeing that they so greatly outnumbered the British ships.

Six small ships ill supplied with fighting men against fifty-three bigger ones filled with soldiers was too great a disparity of force to give even a hope of victory.

And, although Lord Howard would himself have gone into battle even against such odds as that, yet the other commanders were greatly opposed to so rash an enterprise; and the master of his own ship said he would rather jump into the sea than conduct her Majesty's ship and the rest to be a prey to the enemy.

Hence it was that *The Revenge* fought alone on that September day the entire Spanish fleet, and has given us one of the most glorious pages in the annals of our national history.

F. J. Cross

ONE WHO LEFT ALL.

THE STORY OF BISHOP HANNINGTON.

Fancy Hannington, of all persons in the world, turning missionary, and going out to preach the Gospel to the blacks!

It is well-nigh incredible at first thought that such a light-hearted, rollicking, jovial fellow could have given up *everything* for such a work as that!

He had plenty of money, hosts of friends, wife, children, any amount of useful work to do at home, - everything, in fact, that can make life worth living.

What could possibly make such a man as that go into the wilds of Africa to be tormented, tortured, and slain by savages?

I will try and show briefly how it came about.

At school Hannington was the veriest pickle, and was nicknamed "Mad Jim".

On one occasion he lit a bonfire in his dormitory, he pelted the German master with rejected examination papers, and in a single day was caned over a dozen times. Yet he fought the bullies, and kept his word; he was brave, honest and manly, and was a great favourite.

When about fifteen years old he was put into his father's business at Brighton. His life there was certainly not hard or trying. He was allowed to travel a great deal, and thus went over a considerable part of Europe, enjoying himself immensely when so doing. Still, he had no taste for the counting-house; and after six years gave it up to become a clergyman, and forthwith proceeded to Oxford.

Both at Oxford and at Martinhoe, in North Devon, where he spent some time during the vacations, Hannington preserved his reputation for fun and love of adventure. At Oxford he took part in practical jokes innumerable; at Martinhoe cliff-climbing and adventurous scrambles occupied some little of his time.

One day he went with two companions to explore a cave called "The Eyes". Adjoining this they discovered a narrow hole leading to a further cave, which was below high-water mark. Into this with great exertion Jim managed to squeeze himself. It was quite dark inside, and whilst he was describing it to his companions they suddenly noticed that the tide was fast coming in, and implored him to get out of his perilous position at once.

Easier said than done. The difficulty he had found in getting in was a trifle compared with the passage out. He tried head first, then feet first, and whilst his friends tugged he squeezed. It was of no use. The sea had almost reached him, and drowning seemed certain.

F. J. Cross

Then, quite hopeless of escape, he bade his companions good-bye. All at once it occurred to him to try taking off his clothes. This made just the difference required, and with a tremendous effort he got out of his prison-house in the very nick of time.

A little later comes an important entry in his diary: " - opened a correspondence with me to-day, which I speak of as delightful; it led to my conversion".

Thereafter followed a change in Hannington's life - he prayed more.

It seems that about this time a college friend began to think much of him, and to pray earnestly for him; and finally wrote to him a serious, simple, earnest letter, which had much effect on Hannington.

The letter was unanswered for over a year; but coming at a time when the man of twenty-five was beginning to find that there were better things to be done in life than cliff-climbing in the country, or giving pleasant parties at Oxford, it wrought its purpose, and formed the first step towards the new life.

Having spent some time in study, Hannington went up for his ordination examination. He did very well the first day; the second he was ill and could do nothing; the third the same; and when he was dismissed by the bishop he was in a state akin to despair.

The next examination was better, but he was nervous, and found his mind at times a hopeless blank. He passed, but not in such a way as he desired. At the examination for priest's orders he came out at the top of the list.

The first portion of his life as a curate did not seem to point to his making any mark upon his Devonshire flock. His audiences were sleepy, and paid little attention to his sermons.

One day he got lost on Exmoor in trying to make a short cut to a place where he was to conduct service. He was consequently late in arriving, and found the congregation waiting. On explaining why he was late to the clerk: -

"Iss," said that official, "we reckoned you was lost, but now you are here go and put on your surples and be short, for we all want to get back to dinner". Truly he was no Wesley in those days!

But to him, as to every true-hearted seeker, light came at last. Not long afterwards he could write, "I know now that Jesus Christ died for me, and that He is mine and I am His".

After little more than a year in Devonshire, Hannington was appointed curate in charge of St. George's, Hurstpierpoint, near Brighton. By his earnestness he roused the people to a fuller faith and to better works. Finding much drunkenness in the place he turned teetotaler, and persuaded many to sign the pledge. He started Bible classes, prayer meetings, and mothers' meetings. Not only was he a shining light in his own parish, but he also went about the country and assisted at revival missions, showing himself every-where a bright and helpful minister of the Gospel.

In the year 1878 Hannington heard of the violent deaths which had befallen Lieut. Shergold Smith and Mr. O'Neil in Central Africa. From this time he became drawn towards mission work in that district.

It was not, however, till the year 1882 that he finally entered into arrangements with the Church Missionary Society to go to Africa.

Their high estimation of his capacities may be gathered from the fact that he was appointed as leader of the expedition which was being sent out.

It was a horrible wrench at last to leave wife and children. "My most bitter trial," he writes - "an agony that still cleaves to me - was saying good-bye to the little ones. Thank God the pain was all on one side. 'Come back soon, papa!' they cried." His wife had resolutely made up her mind to give him to God, and was brave to the last.

"When at length the ship left England I watched and watched the retreating tow-boat," he continues, "until I could see it no longer, and then hurried down below. Indeed, I felt for the moment as one paralysed. Now is the time for reaction - to 'cast all your care upon Him'."

Strangely enough, both his missionary journeys in Africa failed in their original aim, which was to reach the kingdom of Uganda.

In the first journey the expedition started from the coast at the end of June, 1882. After two months' difficult marching into the interior, amidst the constant difficulties which beset the African traveller, he writes on 1st August: "I am very happy. Fever is trying, but it does not take away the joy of the Lord, and keeps one low in the right place".

On, on they went. Fever was so heavy upon him that his temperature reached 110 degrees; but still he struggled forward, insisting upon placing a weary companion on the beast which he ought himself to have ridden.

By 4th September they reached Uyui, a place which was still far distant from Lake Victoria (or Victoria Nyanza); and now he was at death's door. So intense was the pain he suffered that he asked to be left alone that he might scream, as that seemed to bring some relief.

Notwithstanding this suffering, the expedition started forward again on 16th October, Hannington being placed in a hammock. They reached Lake Victoria, but the leader could go no further. He was utterly broken down by continued fever; and, though the thought of returning to England without accomplishing his mission was bitter to him, it was a necessity.

By June, 1883, he was again in London. How favourable was the impression Hannington had already made upon the Missionary Society is apparent from the fact that the bishopric of East Equatorial Africa was offered him. He was consecrated in June, 1884; and, after visiting Palestine to confirm the churches there, he arrived in Frere Town on the west coast of Africa in January, 1885, and spent several months of useful work in organising. By July, 1885, he was ready to attempt the second time to reach the kingdom of Uganda.

He determined to try a different route from that taken before, in order to avoid the fevers from which the previous expedition had suffered so terribly.

F. J. Cross

After surmounting many difficulties in his passage through Masai Land he had by October reached within a few days' journey of Uganda; but there, on the outskirts of the kingdom he sought to enter, a martyr's death crowned his brief but earnest mission life.

On 21st October, 1885, the bishop had started from his tent to get a view of the river Nile when about twenty of the natives set upon him, robbed him, and hurried him off to prison. He was violently dragged along, some trying to force him one way, some another, dashing him against trees in their hurry, and bruising and wounding him without thought or consideration. Although the bishop believed he was to be thrown over a precipice or murdered at once, he could still say, "Lord, I put myself in Thy hands; I look to Thee alone," and sing, "Safe in the arms of Jesus".

At length, after a journey of about five miles, he was pushed into a hut, and there kept prisoner. Whilst in this place he endured all kinds of horrors. Laughed at in his sufferings by the savages, almost suffocated by the bad smells about the hut, taken out at times to be the sport of his captors, unable to eat, full of aches and pains, he was yet able to look up and say, "Let the Lord do as He sees fit," and to read his Bible and feel refreshed.

On 27th October he writes: "I am very low, and cry to God for release". On the 28th fever developed rapidly. Word was brought that messengers had arrived from Mwanga, King of Uganda. Three soldiers from this monarch had indeed arrived; but, instead of bringing orders for his release, doubtless conveyed instructions that the bishop should be put to death.

It seems that Mwanga had some fear of invasion from the East; and acting on his suspicions, without taking any trouble to ascertain the facts of the case, had sent the fatal command.

On the day of the bishop's release, the 29th, he was held up by Psalm xxx., which came with great power. As he was led forth to execution he sang hymns nearly all the way. When his captors hesitated to launch their spears at him, he spake gently to them and pointed to his gun. So, either by gunshot or spear wounds, died another of that glorious band of martyrs who have, century after century, fearlessly laid down their lives to advance the Kingdom of God.

Mrs. Hannington has kindly made a tracing of the page in the bishop's little pocket diary for 28th October, the day before his martyrdom took place. I am very glad to be able to give a reproduction of so interesting a memento.

Seventh day's prison. Wednesday, 28th October. A terrible night, 1st with noisy, drunken guard, and 2nd with vermin which have found out my tent and swarm. I don't think I got one sound hour's sleep, and woke with fever fast developing. O Lord, do have mercy upon me and release me. I am quite broken down and brought low. Comforted by reading 27th Psalm.

In an hour or two's time fever developing rapidly. My tent was so stifling I was obliged to go inside the filthy hut, and soon was delirious.

Evening: fever passed away. Word came that Mwanga

F. J. Cross

had sent 3 soldiers, but what news they bring they will not yet let me know.

Much comforted by 28th Psalm.

A MAN WHO CONQUERED DISAPPOINTMENTS.

THE STORY OF SIR HENRY HAVELOCK.

He was nicknamed "Phlos" - short for philosopher - even when at school. Havelock and a few companions at Charterhouse met together for devotion, and of course came in for a large amount of jeering from some of the other boys. But it was useless to call him "Methodist" and "hypocrite"; he had learnt from his mother the value of Bible reading, and possessed sufficient character to care little what his companions said.

He knew the right, and did it - thus early he was a philosopher in a small way.

It had been intended that Havelock should follow the law as a profession; and he was studying with this end in view when his father stopped the necessary supplies of money, and he had to turn to some other occupation for a living.

He had always had a leaning towards a military life, and by his brother's aid obtained a commission as second lieutenant in 1815, being then twenty years old.

Unlike Colin Campbell, who was in the thick of the fight within a few months of joining his regiment, it

F. J. Cross

was some years before Havelock had a chance of distinguishing himself; but meantime he set to work to study military history and tactics both ancient and modern.

Not content with this, he learnt Persian and Hindostanee; and thus when he went to India in 1823 he was equipped as few young men of his day were.

Havelock's faith, strong though it was, had to undergo a time of severe trial. Doubts arose in his mind, and made him miserable while they lasted. But on board ship he came across Lieut. Gardner, to whom, with others, he was giving lessons in languages; and as a result of his intercourse with this man he became again the same simple loving believer that he had been when he learnt to read the Bible at his mother's knee, or braved the taunts of his school-fellows.

During the two months he was at Calcutta he held religious meetings, to which the soldiers were invited. At these, not only did he preach the Gospel of Christ, but he made a point of telling the men the blessings of temperance; and it was by his influence that later on a society was formed in the regiment, and various attractions were placed before the men to keep them from intemperance.

Now came the chance of active service for which he had been longing. An expedition was planned against the Burmese, and Havelock was one of the members. But a great disappointment was in store for him. The ship in which he sailed was delayed, and did not arrive at Rangoon till the town was taken. Still, though there was no glory to be gained, there was much good work to be done in looking after his men's comfort and well-being; and this he did to the utmost of his power. He also held simple services, such as the men could appreciate, in one of the Buddhist temples.

Though there was not a great deal of fighting to do, there were great losses of men through disease; and Havelock himself was ere long so ill that he was told a voyage to England was the only thing to save his life.

This, however, he objected to; and after a stay at Bombay he was sufficiently restored to rejoin his regiment.

During this war a night attack was made by the enemy on an outpost; and the men ordered to repulse it were not ready when summoned.

"Then call out Havelock's saints," said the commander-in-chief. "They are always sober, and can be depended upon, and Havelock himself is always ready." And, surely enough, "Havelock's saints" were among the enemy in double quick time, and soon gave them as much steel and lead as they had any wish for!

"Every inch a soldier, and every inch a Christian," - that was an exact description of this man.

Even the day he got married to Hannah Marshman, the missionary's daughter, he showed that he was a soldier before all else. For, having been suddenly summoned to attend a military court of inquiry at twelve o'clock on his wedding day, he got married at an earlier hour than he had previously arranged, took a quick boat to Calcutta, returning to his bride when his business of the day was finished.

F. J. Cross

Time passed on, and the leader of "the saints" was still but a junior lieutenant, though he had been seventeen years in the army. Thrice were his hopes of promotion raised, and thrice doomed to disappointment.

Still he murmured not. "I have only two wishes," he would say. "I pray that in life and death I may glorify God, and that my wife and children may be provided for."

Heavy trials befel him. Death laid its hand on his little boy Ettrick, and another child was so burnt in a fire that happened at their bungalow that he died also, whilst his beloved wife narrowly escaped the same fate. Yet he bore all this with patience.

Stern commander though he was, his men loved him so much that they wanted to give him a month of their pay to assist him in the loss of means occasioned by the fire.

Though their offer was refused, yet Havelock could not but be thankful for the kind feeling which prompted it.

At length, after over twenty years' service, he became a captain.

In the Afghan war Havelock was with General Sale at Jellalabad at the time that Dr. Brydon brought the news of the massacre of our men by the Afghans; and during the anxious time that followed he was able to render good service in the field and at the council table.

He fought in the battles of Moodkee, Ferozeshah, and Sobraon. At the first-named he had two horses shot under him; and in all he distinguished himself by coolness and bravery.

When the terrible mutiny broke out in India in the year 1857, the hour of dire emergency had come, and with it had come the man. "Your excellency," said Sir Patrick Grant, presenting Havelock to Lord Canning, "I have brought the man."

That was on 17th June, 1857.

Two days later Havelock was appointed to the command of the little army. His instructions were that, "after quelling all disturbances at Allahabad, he should not lose a moment in supporting Sir Henry Lawrence at Lucknow, and Sir Hugh Wheeler at Cawnpore; and that he should take prompt measures for dispersing and utterly destroying all mutineers and insurgents".

A large order that to tell a commander with 2000 men, to take a dozen fortified places defended by ten times the number of his own force!

Not a moment was to be lost, for both cities were in deadly peril.

Alas! Early on the 1st July came news of the terrible massacre of the Cawnpore garrison, - men, women and children slain in one wanton, heartless slaughter, which still makes the blood run cold to read about.

Out of the 2000 men under Havelock's command 1400 only were British soldiers. But in that force every man was a hero. Notwithstanding the scorching heat of an Indian summer, - in spite, too, of the fact that a number of the men were obliged to march in heavy garments utterly unsuited to the climate; though death, disease, and a thousand perils lay in front of them, - not a man of Havelock's "Ironsides" but was impatient to push onward to death or victory.

The general himself was full of humble trust in the Lord, and was in good spirits notwithstanding - perhaps because of - the perils before him. For it is written of him that "he was always as sour as if he had swallowed a pint of vinegar except when he was being shot at, - and then he was as blithe as a schoolboy out for a holiday".

Sour he was *not*, but he kept splendid discipline among his troops.

"Soldiers," he said as they set out, "there is work before us. We are bound on an expedition whose object is the supremacy of British rule, and to avenge the fate of British men and women."

The first battle fought was at Futtehpore. Writing to his wife on the same night, Havelock said: "One of the prayers oft repeated throughout my life has been answered, and I have lived to command in a general action.... We fought, and in ten minutes' time the affair was decided.... But away with vain glory! Thanks to God Almighty, who gave me the victory."

Day, after day, the men fought and marched - marched and fought. Battle after battle was won against foes of reckless daring, carefully entrenched, amply supplied with big guns, and infinitely superior in numbers.

His men were often half famished. For two whole days they had but one meal, consisting of a few biscuits and porter!

Hearing that some of the women and children were still alive, having escaped the massacre of 27th June, Havelock pressed on with his wearied little army. "With God's help," said he, "we shall save them, or every man die in the attempt."

Nana Sahib himself barred the way to Cawnpore. His 5000 men were well placed in good positions; but they were driven from post to post before the onset of the British.

"Now, Highlanders!" shouted Havelock, as the men halted to re-form after one of their irresistible onslaughts; "another charge like the last wins the day!"

And again the Scots scattered the enemy, at the bayonet's point.

The sun was far towards the western horizon before the battle was finally over. The mutineers were brave men; and, though beaten, retreated, reformed, and fought again.

The enemy had rallied at a village; and Havelock's men, after their day's fight, lagged a little when, having gone over ploughed fields and swamps, they came again under fire.

But their general rode out under fire of the guns, and, smiling as a cannon ball just missed him by a hairsbreadth, said: -

"Come, who is to take that village - the Highlanders or the 64th?"

That was enough: pell-mell went both regiments upon

the enemy, who had a bad quarter of an hour between the two.

Cawnpore was won; but, alas! the women and children had been slain whilst their countrymen had been fighting for their deliverance. And Lucknow was not yet to be relieved.

For after advancing into Oude Havelock found that constant fighting, cholera, sunstroke and illness had so reduced his numbers that to go on would risk the extermination of his force.

He therefore returned to await reinforcements. By the time these arrived, Sir James Outram had been appointed general of the forces in India; but he generously refused to accept the command till Lucknow had been relieved, saying that, Havelock having made such noble exertions, it was only right he should have the honour of leading the troops till this had been done.

So he accompanied the army as a volunteer; and again the men fought their way, this time right through the mutineers, accomplishing their object by the first relief of Lucknow.

On the evening of 28th September, the soldiers reached the Residency, where the British had been shut up for so long face to face with death. The last piece of fighting was the worst they had had to face. Fired at from roof and window by concealed foes, they marched on with unwavering courage, and those who reached the Residency had a reward such as can come to few in this life.

As the women and children frantic with joy rushed to

welcome their rescuers the stern-set faces of the Highlanders changed to joy and gladness; hunger, thirst, wounds, weariness - all were forgotten as they clasped hands with those for whom they had fought and bled.

"God bless you," they exclaimed; "why, we expected to have found only your bones!"

"And the children living too!"

Women and children, civilians and soldiers, gave themselves up to pure gladness of heart, and in that meeting all thought of past woes and dangers faded away.

After a series of the most thrilling incidents the world has known, Lucknow was finally relieved by Sir Colin Campbell.

When Havelock came from the Residency to meet the troops the men flocked round him cheering, and their enthusiasm brought tears to the veteran's eyes.

On the 17th November Lucknow was relieved, and on the 24th Havelock died. "I have," he said to Outram in his last illness, "for forty years so ruled my life that when death came I might face it without fear."

A FRIEND OF PRISONERS.

THE STORY OF JOHN HOWARD.

In St. Paul's Cathedral there stands a monument representing a man with a key in his right hand and a scroll in his left, whilst on the pedestal from which he looks down are pictured relics of the prison life of the past. The man is John Howard, who travelled tens of thousands of miles, and spent many years in visiting gaols all over England and the Continent, and in endeavouring to render prison life less degrading and brutalising. Wherever he went prison doors were unlocked as if he possessed a magic key; and by his life and books he did more to help prisoners than any other man.

It is only just over a hundred years since John Howard died; yet in his day persons could be put to death for stealing a horse or a sheep, for robbing dwellings, for defrauding creditors, for forgery, for wounding deer, for killing or maiming cattle, for stealing goods to the value of five shillings, or even for cutting a band in a hop plantation. And many persons who were innocent of any offence would lie in dungeons for years!

At his father's death John Howard came into possession of a good property; and, marrying a lady some years older than himself, settled down on his estate and passed three years of quiet happiness.

Then a great grief came to him. His wife died, and Howard was bowed down with sorrow.

But the distress brought with it a longing to be a comfort to others; and he set out for Lisbon, which had just been visited by the great earthquake of 1755, with the hope of assisting the homeless and suffering.

France and England were then at war, and on his way thither he was captured by a French vessel and thrown into prison. He was placed in a dark, damp, filthy dungeon, and was half starved. For two months he was kept a prisoner, and as soon as he was free he set about obtaining the release of his fellow captives.

Some years later he became a sheriff of Bedford, and began visiting the prisoners in the gaol where John Bunyan wrote the *Pilgrim's Progress*.

From the inquiries he made during the course of his visitations he was astonished to find that the gaolers received no salary, and that they lived on what they could make out of the prisoners. As a result it often happened that those who had been acquitted at their trial were kept in prison long afterwards, because they were unable to pay the fees which the gaoler demanded.

Horrified at the state in which he found the prison and at the abuses of justice that prevailed, John Howard determined to find out what was done in other parts of the kingdom, and visited a number of gaols throughout the country. And fearful places he found them to be! Boys who were taken to gaol for the first time were put

F. J. Cross

with old and hardened criminals; the prisons were dirty and ill-smelling; the dungeons were dark and unhealthy; and, unless prisoners could afford to pay for comforts, they were obliged to sleep on cold bare floors, even delicate women not being exempted from such cruel treatment.

At Exeter he found two sailors in gaol, having been fined one shilling each for some trifling offence, and owing £1 15s. 8d. for fees to the gaolers and clerk of the peace. When he visited Cardiff he heard a man had just died in prison after having been there ten years for a debt of seven pounds. At Plymouth he found that three men had been shut up in a little dark room only five and a half feet high, so that they could neither breathe freely nor stand upright.

Hundreds of cases as bad or worse than these did he discover and bring before public notice.

He gave evidence before the House of Commons of what he had seen. Then Acts of Parliament were passed, providing that gaolers should be paid out of the rates, that prisoners who were found not guilty should be set at liberty at once, that the prisons should be kept clean and healthy, and the prisoners properly clothed and attended to.

Determined that these Acts should not remain a dead letter, he went about the country seeing that what Parliament required was actually carried out.

Not contented with what he had already done, he travelled abroad, inspecting the prisons of France, Russia, Holland, Switzerland, Germany, and other countries, in order to see how they compared with those in Great Britain.

Strange to say, he discovered that in a number of cases they were in many ways better; and the prisoners, unlike their fellows in Britain, were generally employed in some useful manner.

When he was in London on one occasion he heard that there had been a revolt in the military prison in the Savoy. Two of the gaolers had been killed, and the rioters held possession of the building. Howard set off for the prison, though he was warned that his life would not be safe if he ventured inside. Nothing daunted, he went amongst the prisoners, and soon persuaded them to go back to their cells peaceably, promising to bring their grievances before the authorities.

At Paris he was unable for a long time to get into that great prison house which then existed called the Bastille. Try as he would, he could gain no admittance. One day when he was passing he went to the gate of the prison, rang the bell and marched in. After passing the sentry he stopped and took a good look at the building, then he had to beat a hasty retreat, and narrowly escaped capture; but by that time he had partly accomplished his object.

When Howard was in Russia the empress sent a message saying she desired to see him; but he returned an answer that he was devoting his time to inspecting prisons, and had no leisure for visiting the palaces of rulers.

At Rome, however, he was prevailed on to go and see the Pope, on the express understanding that he should not be obliged to kiss his holiness's toe; and he came away with a very pleasant remembrance of the Holy Father.

At Vienna the Emperor Joseph II. specially requested an interview. Howard refused at first to meet the emperor's wishes; but, on the English ambassador representing good might come of the visit, Howard went to see his majesty, and remained with him two hours in conversation, during which time he made the emperor acquainted with the bad state of some of the Austrian prisons. Once or twice the emperor was angered by Howard's plainness of speech, but told the ambassador afterwards that he liked the prison reformer all the better for his honesty.

Having made up his mind to see the quarantine establishment at Marseilles, Howard made his way through France, though he was so feared and disliked by the Government that he was warned if he were caught in that country he would be thrown into the Bastille.

He disguised himself as a doctor, and after some narrow escapes arrived at Marseilles and visited the Lazaretto (or place of detention for the infected), though even Frenchmen were forbidden to do so. He took drawings of the place, and then went on a tour to many southern cities. He was at Smyrna while fever was raging with fury, and went amongst the sick and fever-stricken, fearless of the consequences.

In the course of his travels the ship in which he was a passenger was attacked by pirates, and John Howard showed himself as brave in actual battle as he was in fighting abuses; for he loaded the big gun with which the ship was armed nearly up to the muzzle with nails and spikes, and fired it into the pirate crew just in time to save himself and his companions from destruction. The books in which he gave an account of his experiences were eagerly read by the public, and produced a profound effect.

His last journey was to Russia. At Cherson he received an urgent request to visit a lady who had the fever. The place where she lived was many miles off, and no good horses were to be obtained. But he was determined not to disappoint her; so he procured a dray horse and started for his destination on a wintry night, with rain falling in torrents. As a result of this journey he was stricken down by the fever, and died 20th January, 1790.

Howard was a very hard worker, and a man of most frugal habits. He was often up by two o'clock in the morning writing and doing business till seven, when he breakfasted. He ate no flesh food, and drank no wine or spirits. He had a great dislike to any fuss being made about him personally; and, though £1500 was subscribed during his life to erect a memorial, it was, at his earnest desire, either returned to the subscribers or spent in assisting poor debtors.

But after his death a memorial was put up in St. Paul's, and quite recently a monument has been erected at Bedford, where he first began his labours on behalf of the prisoners.

A HERO OF THE VICTORIA CROSS.

THE STORY OF KAVANAGH.

It was the time of the Indian Mutiny. Lucknow was in the hands of the rebels. Within the Residency Sir James Outram, Sir Henry Havelock, and their troops, were fast shut up, around them a vast multitude of mutineers. But now near at hand was Sir Colin Campbell with the army of relief.

It was difficult, nay, almost impossible, to get a trusty messenger through that multitude of fierce and blood-thirsty foes; and yet it was of the utmost importance that Sir Colin should have some one to tell him what was passing within the Residency, and show him the best route by which his troops could approach.

If any man tried to get through and failed, death - or perhaps worse still, horrible torture - was his certain fate. But there was one man who determined to do it, or die in the attempt. His name was Kavanagh. It was so dangerous a matter that when Sir James Outram heard of his proposal he declared he would not have asked one of his officers to attempt the passage. But in the end he accepted the offer, and Kavanagh prepared for the journey.

Dressing himself as a native soldier, and covering his

face and hands with lampblack, he was so altered in appearance that even his friends failed to recognise him. Thus disguised, and accompanied by a native spy named Kunoujee Lal to guide him, he set out. The night, fortunately, was dark and favoured their design. The first thing they did was to ford the Goomtee, a river about a hundred yards wide, and four or five feet deep. Taking off their garments they waded across; but whilst in the water Kavanagh's courage reached a low ebb, and he wished himself back again. However, they got to the opposite bank in safety, and crouching up a ditch found a grove of trees, where they dressed.

Kavanagh's confidence had now returned, and he felt so sure of his disguise that he even exchanged a few words with a matchlock-man whom they met. After going on for about half a mile they reached the iron bridge over the river, and here they were challenged by a native officer. Kavanagh kept judiciously in the shade whilst the guide advanced and answered the questions put to him satisfactorily, and they were allowed to proceed. A little further they passed through a number of Sepoys, but these let them go by without inquiry. Having had the good fortune to get unperceived past a sentry who was closely questioning a native, they came into the principal street of Lucknow, jostling against the armed rebels, who would have killed them in a moment had their suspicion been aroused. But no mishap occurred, and after being challenged by a watchman they at last found themselves to their great relief out in the open country.

They were now in the best of spirits, and went along for a few miles in a state of great gladness. Then came a rude shock. They had taken the wrong direction, and were returning into the midst of the rebels. It was an awful awakening for Kavanagh. Suppose the spy after all were playing him false. It seemed an extraordinary mistake to have made. Happily it was stupidity not treason that had caused the disastrous loss of time, and the guide was full of sorrow for his error.

There was nothing now to be done but to return as quickly as possible; but they were for a while in an awkward fix, as they could get no one to direct them.

A man whom they asked declared he was too old to guide them, another on being commanded to lead them ran off shouting and alarmed the village. It was now midnight, so there was no time to be lost. They made for the canal, into which Kavanagh fell several times, for his shoes were wet and slippery, and he was footsore and weary. By this time the shoes he wore had rubbed the skin off his toes and cut into the flesh above the heels.

About two o'clock in the morning they came across a picket of Sepoys, and, thinking it safer not to try and avoid them, went up and asked the way. Having answered the inquiries put to them without exciting suspicion, they were directed aright.

They now made for Sir Colin's camp, which the spy told him was situated at a village called Bunnee, about eighteen miles from Lucknow. The moon had risen by this time, and they could now see their way clearly. About three o'clock a villager observing them approach called out a Sepoy guard of twenty-five men, who asked them all kinds of questions. Kunoujee Lal now got frightened, for the first time; and threw away the letter he had received, for fear of being taken, but Kavanagh kept his in his turban. At last they satisfied the guard that they were poor men travelling to the village of Umroola to inform a friend of the death of his brother, and they were directed on their perilous road.

Hardly had they got through one difficulty than they were into another. For now they found themselves in a swamp, where they waded for two hours up to their waists in water. This might have proved the worst accident of all, for in forcing his way through the weeds nearly all the black was washed off Kavanagh's hands. Had they after this been seen by the enemy there would have been little chance of either of them reaching the British lines alive.

Much against the spy's advice, Kavanagh now insisted on a quarter of an hour's rest, for he was about worn out. After this they passed between two of the enemy's pickets who, happily for them, had no sentries thrown out, and reached a grove of trees. Here he asked Kunoujee Lal to see if there was any one who could tell them where they were. Before they had gone far, however, they heard with joy the English challenge, "Who goes there?" They had reached a British cavalry outpost, and Kavanagh's eyes filled with tears as he shook the officer's hand. They took him into a tent, gave him some dry clothes and refreshment; and he thanked God for having preserved him through the perils of that awful night.

All through the British camp spread the tale of Kavanagh's brave deed; and the enthusiasm of officers and men alike knew no bounds.

The information he was able to give proved of the greatest assistance; and a little later he had the honour of conducting Sir James Outram and Sir Henry Havelock into the presence of Sir Colin Campbell, and witnessed the meeting of these three great commanders.

When the army of relief forced its way into Lucknow, Kavanagh was always near the commander-in-chief; and, when at length they drew near to the besieged, he was one of the first at the Residency, and as he approached a loud cheer burst forth from his old associates. "It is Kavanagh!" they shouted. "He is the first to relieve us. Three cheers for him!"

In consideration of his gallant services he received the Victoria Cross, and was afterwards made Assistant-Commissioner of Oude.

THE MAN WHO BRAVED THE FLOOD.

THE STORY ON CAPTAIN LENDY'S BRAVE DEED.

In the autumn of 1893 a police force of forty men, under the command of Captain E.A.W. Lendy, Inspector-General of Police, in Sierra Leone, was sent to open a road to Koinadugu, which, owing to the war with the Sofas, had been closed.

It was no easy task to perform. The men had to cut their way through a dense jungle. This was heavy and tiring work, and, owing to the fact that for a month past they had been obliged to exist on a small quantity of rice, they were not in the best condition to undertake such labour.

However, so as to get the road finished as quickly as possible they worked from sunrise to sunset. Even the night slid not bring them rest and peace; for the rain descended in such a manner as to add to the discomfort of their situation.

On the 4th of November the force arrived at the Sell or Roquelle river. The stream was eighty yards wide. There was no bridge over it, but only a creeper rope tied across from bank to bank.

F. J. Cross

The river was very full, and a swift current was running; two hundred yards below, the noise of falls sounded a warning note, and it was known that alligators infested the district.

No wonder, then, that the natives were terrified at the idea of attempting to swim across.

Yet the river lay between Captain Lendy's force and the food and rest it needed. So, though owing to the privations the men had endured their vital powers were at a low ebb, yet, with starvation staring them in the face they must make the passage - alligators and falls notwithstanding.

The first to cross were two policemen, who, after a difficult journey, got safe to the other side.

Then followed a scene of excitement and danger. Private Momo Bangura and Sergeant Smith were the next pair to start. Hardly had they reached midstream when Bangura's rifle band, slipping over his arms, pinned them to his side.

Smith gallantly went to the rescue; but it was difficult enough for him to get along alone; and, with Bangura to support, he quickly became exhausted. After shouting for help, he and his companion disappeared from view beneath the waters.

At once two other men went to Bangura's assistance, giving Smith an opportunity of looking to his own safety.

But it seemed a hopeless struggle. Worn by their previous exertions, the men were unable to give any permanent help to Bangura, and were in their turn dragged under several times in their efforts to afford him assistance. Indeed, it now seemed that, in spite of all the bravery shown, Bangura's fate was sealed, if not that of his would-be rescuers also.

It was a terrible predicament. Four men were struggling in the seething waters in deadly danger. Too brave and resolute to leave their comrade-in-arms, too feeble to procure his safety, they were wearing out their strength in futile though heroic efforts, whilst the object of their solicitude was at his last gasp.

At this moment their brave commander came to the rescue, and at once changed the aspect of affairs.

Diving into the stream he soon reached the drowning man; and the others, released from their burden, were now able to give their undivided attention to self-preservation.

The supreme moment had arrived. Would Captain Lendy's efforts end as the others had done? If so, it is probable that all would have found a watery grave in the Roquelle; for, exhausted though they were, the three other men were far too fond of their commander to have left him to perish alone.

It was for a time a stern fight with death. But Lendy was cool, calm, resourceful. Yard by yard the distance between the further shore was lessened, notwith-standing the race of the waters toward the falls. Foot by foot he drew nearer to safety, though the man lay like a log in the grasp of his rescuer, unable to assist in the struggle that was going on.

At length the shadow of death was dissipated; for the gallant soldier managed to land his burden on the further shore, which the others had already reached.

The end of the stern combat with the waters was particularly gratifying, as several men had previously lost their lives in crossing the same river.

The silver medal of the Royal Geographical Society was awarded to Captain Lendy, and a bronze medal given to his brave followers.

But, alas! Lendy did not live to receive his medal. Ere it could reach him he had fallen in a night attack which the French made by mistake upon our forces, supposing them to be natives whom they were seeking to punish. Ere the error was discovered the loss on both sides was serious, and in the conflict her Majesty was deprived of the services of a devoted and faithful servant by the death of heroic Captain E.A.W. Lendy.

The little block in this page is a reproduction of Momo Bangura's statement forwarded to the Colonial Office, duly witnessed by his companions' signatures.

Pte Momo. Bangurah's Statement.

My name is Pte Momo Bangurah. I am a private in the Frontier Police Force. On the 4th instant I tried to cross over the Seli River. I slung my rifle across my shoulder half way across, the sling slipped and so I could not use my arms. I sank but Sergeant Smith caught me. I dragged him down twice and called out for help. Corporal Sambah and Parkins then kept me up but the stream was so strong, that we were taken under several times. I thought my last moment had come. I remember Captain Lendy seizing me and then I forgot everything till I found myself being rubbed on shore. If it had not been for Captain Lendy Sergeant Smith Corporals Samba and Parkins, I know I should have been drowned and I thank them for their assistance.

(sd) Momo Bangur

his mark.

Witnesses

(sd) Benoni Johnson Sub Inspr. F.P.
" R.W. Sawyer Sergt
" S. Jenkins Coker Sergt
" Emanuel R. Palmer Sergt

A TEMPERANCE LEADER.

THE STORY OF JOSEPH LIVESEY.

The leader of the great temperance movement in England - Joseph Livesey, of Preston - had a very bad start in life.

He was quite poor; he lost both father and mother from consumption when he reached his eighth year; he was frail and delicate; his brothers and sisters all died young; so that he seemed ill fitted to make any headway in the race of life.

His grandfather, who adopted him, failed in business; and Joseph Livesey commenced his career by doing the work of a domestic servant, as well as toiling at the loom.

"As we were too poor to keep a servant," he says, "and having no female help except to wash the clothes and occasionally clean up, I may be said to have been the housekeeper."

But, whilst he was weaving in the cellar where his grandfather and uncle also worked, he was at the same time gaining knowledge day by day.

When his pocket money of a penny a week was

increased to threepence, he felt himself on the high road to wealth, and ere long he was the possessor of a Bible and a grammar, which he set himself to study whenever he could get a spare moment.

One can scarcely realise the difficulties that lay in the way of a studious boy in those days. A newspaper cost sevenpence; there were no national schools or Sunday schools, no penny publications, no penny postage, no railways, no gas, and no free libraries, and no free education! Yet so resolute was he in his desire for education that, though he was not even allowed a candle after the elders went to bed, he would sit up till late at night reading by the glow of the embers.

It is sad enough to see the number of families that are ruined by drink at the present time; but in Livesey's early days people suffered even more from drunkenness than they do now.

The weavers used to keep Monday as a day of leisure; and the public-houses were crowded from morning till night with men and women, who drank away their earnings to the last penny.

In the church to which Joseph Livesey belonged the ringers and singers were hard drinkers, the gravedigger was a drunkard, and the parish clerk was often intoxicated!

Living amidst so much sin and misery, this frail lad determined to strive his hardest to assist others. He found Sunday a day of rest and rejoicing to him "a feast of good things," and became a Sunday-school teacher and preacher.

F. J. Cross

So far as worldly matters went he was not at all successful in early life. Weaving was so badly paid that he tried several other trades, but only to meet with failure.

At the age of twenty he received a legacy of a few pounds; and soon after, having saved a little money, married a good and true woman, who helped him much throughout life.

"Our cottage," says Mr. Livesey in his autobiography, "though small, was like a palace; for none could excel my Jenny for cleanliness and order. I renovated the garden, and made it a pleasant place to walk in. On the loom I was most industrious, working from early in the morning often till ten, and sometimes later, at night; and she not only did all the house work, but wound the bobbins for three weavers - myself, uncle, and grand-father; and yet, with all this apparently hard lot, these were happy days."

But it was not all sunshine at first. He fell ill, and the doctor ordered him better living than he had been getting; and where the money was to come from to get more nourishing food Livesey knew not.

He had been ordered to take some cheese in the forenoon, so he bought a piece at about eightpence a pound; and as he munched it came this thought: cheese wholesale cost but fivepence per pound; would it not be possible to buy a piece wholesale and sell it to his friends, so that he too might have the benefit of getting it at this low price?

No sooner thought of than done. But, when he had finished weighing out the cheese to his friends, he found he had made, quite unexpectedly, a profit of eighteenpence, and that it was more than he could have gained by a great deal of weaving.

So he changed his trade: weaving gave place to cheese mongering; and, after some very hard work and persevering efforts, he placed himself beyond the reach of poverty.

Now came the important moment of his life. One day in settling a bargain he drank a glass of whisky. It was, he said, the best he ever drank, because it was the last. For the sensation it produced made him resolve he would never again taste a drop of intoxicating liquor.

Finding himself the better for this course, he soon tried to get others to join him. His first convert to *total abstinence* was a man named John King; Livesey and he signed together; and on 1st September, 1832, at a meeting held at Preston, seven men - "the Seven Men of Preston," as they are called - signed the pledge, of which the following is a facsimile: -

[Handwritten: We agree to *abstain* from all Liquors of an *Intoxicating Quality*, whether ale porter Wine, or Ardent Spirits, except as Medicine.

John Gratix
Edw'd Dickinson
Jno: Broadbelt
Jno: Smith
Joseph Livesey
David Anderson
Jno: Ring.]

It was a terrible struggle for these men at first. They

were laughed at, they were abused, they were persecuted; but the more people tried to put them down the harder they fought; and soon hundreds and thousands had joined their ranks, and the movement spread throughout the kingdom.

"There is more food in a pennyworth of bread," said Livesey, "than in a gallon of ale"; and he proved it. He lectured far and wide; and, though he met with much opposition, facts in the end prevailed.

He was not only a temperance advocate, but an earnest worker for the good of others in various directions. He visited the sick, and helped them. When the railways came he started cheap trips to the seaside for working people, and was never happier than when he was helping the poor and unfortunate.

Joseph Livesey is a striking example of the benefits to health derived from teetotalism, as he lived to the good old age of ninety.

A GREAT MISSIONARY EXPLORER.

THE STORY OF DAVID LIVINGSTONE.

It is past ten o'clock at night. A little boy fond of going about the country in search of plants has returned home. Finding the door of his father's house locked, and fearing to awaken his parents, he settles down contentedly on the step to spend the night there. Then a woman's hand quietly unbolts the door and receives the little wanderer back. The boy is David Livingstone. Now-a-days we know him as one of the greatest missionary explorers of our times.

A stern father, a loving mother, both godly and upright people - such were the parents of David; and he respected and loved them with a true and constant affection.

The boy was fond of learning - so fond indeed that when he was at the factory he would keep his book open before him on the spinning machine. Most people think "one thing at a time" is a very good maxim - David thought two things at a time was even better.

At home he was ever ready to lend a hand at house work to save his mother. "If you bar the door, mother," he would say, "I'll wash the floor;" and wash the floor he did, times without number!

F. J. Cross

In later life he used to say he was glad he had thus toiled; and that, if it were possible to begin life again, he would like to go through just the same hard training.

He got on quickly at lessons, and became, like his father, a total abstainer for life. He was fond of serious books; and, reading the lives of Christian missionaries, he began to wish to be one himself. Ere long he journeyed from Blantyre near Glasgow (where he had been working as a factory hand) to London, to prepare for going abroad as a missionary.

His first address was not very promising. He gave out his text, and then was obliged to confess that his sermon had quite gone out of his mind.

In the year 1840 David Livingstone, being then just over twenty-seven years old, went out to South Africa as a missionary. He made his way up country to the furthest district in which the London Missionary Society then had a station. There he taught the Hottentots, and his heart was ere long rejoiced by the change which took place in them.

Before leaving home he had studied medicine, and passed his examination satisfactorily; and this know-ledge of healing he found most useful. His patients, the poor African blacks, would walk a hundred miles to seek his advice, and his waggon was followed by a great crowd of sick folk anxious to be healed.

He studied the language of the tribes amongst whom he was ministering; and soon the people were able to sing in their own tongue, "There is a fountain filled with blood," "Jesus shall reign where'er the sun," and other beautiful hymns which delight the hearts of those in our own land.

Whilst he was gaining the affection of the natives, he did not forget his loved ones at home; and out of his scanty salary of about £100 a year he sent £20 to his parents.

Before he had been long in Africa he had an adventure which nearly cost him his life. In the parts where he was teaching, the lions were very troublesome, and would come by night and seize cattle. Sometimes even they would venture into the gardens and carry off women and children. So the people got together an expedition to go and hunt the lions, and Livingstone joined them. After they had been on the track for some time, and several lions had escaped owing to the fright of the natives, Livingstone saw one sitting on a rock about thirty yards off. He took careful aim and fired both barrels of his gun, wounding it badly.

The people thought it was, dead, and were going towards it, but Livingstone made them keep back and began reloading. Before he had finished, the lion sprang upon him, caught him by the shoulder, and began shaking and tearing him so badly that he was utterly overcome. Two persons who tried to help him were bitten by the lion. But just when it looked as if the missionary's life had reached its last day, the lion suddenly fell down dead from the effect of the bullets which he had fired into it.

Four years after he had been in Africa he married Mary Moffat, the missionary's daughter. She was a true helpmate, and in the trials and difficulties which beset him his way was made clearer and brighter by this good and loving woman.

F. J. Cross

He could not always take his wife with him, as the districts he explored were so wild and savage. He ran risks of death by thirst, by hostile tribes and disease, and went through terrible places where no woman could have lived. But on many a long and perilous journey she went with him. "When I took her," writes Livingstone, "on two occasions to Lake Ngami and far beyond, she endured more than some who have written large books of travel."

One of Livingstone's first mission stations was Mabotsa, where he stayed a year, and in that short time gained the love of the people. When he thought it well to move on farther north the natives offered to build him a new house, schools, anything he wished if he would only stay.

But he had made up his mind that it was best to go to fresh districts rather than stay in places where there were already teachers, and therefore proceeded forty miles further on to Chonuane. Here he met with almost immediate success. The chief, Sechele by name, became a convert and was able in a few weeks to read the Bible. Isaiah was his favourite book. "He was a fine man, that Isaiah," remarked Sechele; "he knew how to speak."

This chief would have been willing to help Livingstone to convert his tribe at a great pace, only his method was not to the missionary's liking.

"Do you think," said Sechele, "you can make my people believe by talking to them? I can make them do nothing except by thrashing them, and if you like I shall call my headman, and with our whips of rhinoceros hide we will soon make them all believe together!"

Like all missionaries, Livingstone was doomed to suffer disappointments. Thus after labouring at Kolobeng for ten years the Boers, annoyed with him for endeavouring to teach them that the natives should be treated with kindness and consideration, made an attack on his house when he was absent. They slaughtered a number of the men and women, carried away 200 children into slavery, and burnt down the mission station. Livingstone was deeply grieved about the capture of the children, but as to his own loss he merely says: "The Boers by taking possession of all my goods have saved me the trouble of making a will".

Still on, on into the dark continent went Livingstone. Not dark to him, for he loved the natives and possessed such powers of attraction that wherever he settled he won their affections.

After taking leave of Sechele he travelled several hundred miles to the territory of Sebituane.

On the road Livingstone and his family had a terribly anxious time. The water in the waggons was all but finished, they were passing through a desert land, their guide had left them. The children were suffering from thirst; his wife, though not uttering a word of reproach, was in an agony of anxiety for her little ones, and Livingstone was fearful lest they should perish in this desert country. When hope had nearly vanished some of the party who had gone out searching for water returned with a supply. They were soon after welcomed by Sebituane, the greatest chief in Central Africa, who gave them food to eat, soft skins to lie upon, and made much of them.

After the death of Sebituane his son Sekeletu was equally friendly, as may be gathered from this page of Livingstone's diary, which, by the kindness of his daughter, Mrs. Bruce, I am permitted to reproduce.

This entry in his diary was written on the eve of Livingstone's great journey to the West Coast. Having sent his wife and family to England, he determined to find a way from the centre of Africa to the West Coast. It was a forlorn hope; but, says Livingstone, "Cannot the love of Christ carry the missionary where the slave trade carries the trader? I shall open up a path to the interior or perish."

On the 11th of November, 1853, he left Linyante, having overcome Sekeletu's objection to let him go, and arrived at Loando, on the West Coast, on 31st May, 1854, after a variety of adventures, and being reduced by fever to a mere skeleton.

The sight of the sea, which gladdened Livingstone's heart, astonished his native escort beyond description. "We were marching along with our father," they said, "believing that what the ancients had told us was true - that the world had no end; but all at once the world said to us, 'I am finished, there is no more of me'."

At Loando friends tried to persuade Livingstone to go to England by sea, but he had promised Sekeletu to return with the men who accompanied him on his great journey, and would not be turned from his purpose. And he arrived at Linyante on the return journey with every one of the 27 men he had taken with him safe and sound!

After this followed the journey to the East Coast

ending at Quilemane.

Besides discovering several large lakes, Livingstone was the first to see the Falls of the Zambesi, which he named the Victoria Falls, after her Majesty the Queen. The water at these falls dashes down in torrents, a sheer depth of 320 feet, the spray rises mountains high and can be seen many miles away, whilst its sound is like the noise of thunder.

Numerous were the expeditions he made. In the course of these he traversed thousands of miles of country before untrodden by the feet of Europeans. His fame had now spread to the four quarters of the globe, and he had published several volumes giving an account of his explorations.

In January, 1873, he started on his last journey. In April, after suffering intensely from constant illness, he got to a place near Lake Bemba; and here he told his followers to build a hut for him to die in. On the 27th April he wrote the last entry in his diary, viz., "Knocked up quite, and remain - recover - sent to buy milch cows. We are on the banks of the Molilamo." When on the 1st May his followers went into the hut they found the great explorer kneeling by his bedside - dead.

Great was their grief and great was the sorrow of all in this country when the news reached Britain of his decease.

But the little factory boy had done such a great work that no place was good enough for his remains but Westminster Abbey.

FROM FARM LAD TO MERCHANT PRINCE.

THE STORY OF GEORGE MOORE.

George Moore was born in Cumberland in 1807. His father was a small farmer. He had the misfortune to lose his mother when he was six years old; but his father was a good and pious man, whose example had a great effect upon him.

The lad was shrewd and earnest, and showed a power of thinking and acting for himself.

At one time he worked for his brother in return for his board and lodging; but wishing to make some money for himself he asked the neighbouring farmers to give him some extra work to do, for which he got wages.

By the time he was ten years old he was able to earn as much as eighteenpence a day, and at twelve years old did the work and earned the wages of a full-grown man.

He had had but little schooling, and his master was one of those persons who thought the best way to get learning implanted in a boy's mind was by forcing it into him at the point of the ruler. He beat his boys much, but taught them little.

To finish his education his father sent George for one quarter to a better school. The cost was only eight shillings, but the boy then got an idea for the first time of the value of learning.

He determined not to return to farm life, believing he could do better for himself in a town. So at about thirteen years of age George Moore began his business life as apprentice to a draper at Wigton.

He did not make at all a pleasant or successful start. His work was very hard. He had to light fires, clean windows, groom horses, and make himself generally useful. His master was fond of drink, and George had to get his meals at a public-house. One of his duties was to serve out spirits to customers who made good purchases.

All things considered, it is perhaps not surprising that he got into bad habits himself. He began to gamble at cards, sitting up often nearly all night, and losing or winning considerable sums of money.

At last a change came in a rather unexpected manner. George lodged at his master's house, and when he went out to play was accustomed to leave a window unfastened so that he could let himself in without rousing the household. Somehow or other his master found out this plan, and determined to put a stop to it. So one night when George had gone out he nailed down the window, and when the apprentice returned home in the early hours of the morning he found himself locked out. Nothing daunted he climbed on to the roof and managed to get in through his bedroom window.

F. J. Cross

But he narrowly escaped being discharged, and on thinking the matter over he saw how great was his folly. So he determined, with God's help, to give up his evil ways, and was enabled to lead a better life in future.

As soon as his apprenticeship was up George Moore resolved to try his fortune in London. At first everything went against him. He tramped the streets of the city from morn till eve, calling here, there and everywhere, seeking for employment, and finding no one to give him a trial. At last he made up his mind to go to America. One day, however, he received from a Cumberland man engaged in the drapery trade a request to call upon him. To his intense delight he was engaged, receiving a salary of thirty pounds a year.

George had now got his foot on the first round of the ladder, and made up his mind to climb higher. So he at once took lessons at a night school, and worked hard at self-education.

Then he got a better place; but, for a time, had to bear much abuse from his master, who declared that, although he had come across many blockheads from Cumberland, George was the stupidest one of all! Still he bore the reproaches of his employer good-naturedly, and before long made his mark. He was offered the position of town traveller, and soon proved himself to be one of the cleverest business men of the time.

Before this, however, George had made up his mind about marriage. Seeing his master's little daughter come into the shop he was much struck by her appearance, and remarked that, if he were ever able to marry, that girl should be his wife. His companions laughed at him heartily; but, as a matter of fact, he did marry that girl, though she refused him the first time he asked.

From this it will be seen that George Moore was no ordinary youth; and before he had been travelling for his firm long, they discovered his value. So did another firm, which found he was taking away their business, and offered him £500 a year to travel for them. But George told them nothing less than a partnership would satisfy him; and as they were determined to secure his services they gave it him, and at the age of twenty-three George Moore became junior partner in the famous house of Groucock & Copestake, to which the name of Moore was then added.

His fortune was thus early made, and his business life was one continued series of successes. He had an immense capacity for work, and boasted that for twelve years he laboured sixteen hours a day.

Yet his energies were not confined to business. After a time, when he no longer needed to work so hard for himself, he took up various charitable schemes, and by his intense vigour soon obtained for them remarkable support. The Commercial Travellers' Schools was one of the institutions in which he took great interest. These schools were built at a cost of about £25,000, the greater portion of which he obtained.

In his native county, in his house of business; everywhere George Moore became famed for his liberal gifts. He spent £15,000 in building a church in one of the poorest districts of London. He visited Paris just after the siege to assist in the distribution of the funds subscribed in England; and to many charitable schemes he subscribed with a generous hand.

In November, 1876, he was knocked down in the streets of Carlisle by a runaway horse, and carried into the hospital to die. He had expressed a wish when he was in good health to be told when he was dying; so his wife said to him, "We have often talked about heaven. Perhaps Jesus is going to take you home. You are willing to go with Him, are you not?"

"Yes," he replied; "I fear no evil ... He will never leave me, nor forsake me."

A MAN WHO ASKED AND RECEIVED.

THE STORY OF GEORGE MÜLLER.

In the year 1805 was born in Prussia George Müller, whose orphanages at Ashley Down, Bristol, may be regarded as one of the modern wonders of the world.

His father intended that George should become a minister, but the lad in his early days showed no signs of a desire to set apart his life to good works. He had the misfortune to lose his mother when he was fourteen years old, and though he was confirmed in 1820 no deep impression had been made by God's grace in his heart.

When he was sixteen he went to Brunswick, and putting up at an hotel lived expensively, and had to part with his best clothes to pay the bill. Later on, for leaving an hotel without paying, he was put in prison, and had to stay there till the money was sent for his release.

He had, indeed, grown so hardened that he could tell lies without blushing. He pretended to lose some money which had been sent to him, and his friends gave him more to replace it. He got into debt, and pawned his clothes in order to procure the means to go to taverns and places of amusement.

F. J. Cross

But the hand of God was upon him, and he did not do these things without suffering in his mind. About this time too he began to study the Bible earnestly.

At the age of twenty the great change came. He attended a prayer meeting, and there his eyes became opened, and he saw there was no hope for him but in Christ. He read the Bible anew, and from that time commenced leading a *new life*.

When he was about twenty-four years old Müller came over to England, and settled at Teignmouth as pastor of a small church. He refused to have any regular salary or to receive pew rents, taking only such offerings as his congregation wished to give him. Sometimes he had no money left at all; at others he had only just enough food for one meal, and knew not where the means were coming from for the next. Yet he trusted entirely in God, and was never left in want.

After this he went to Bristol, and seeing many poor children uncared for laid the matter before God; and, believing it to be His will that he should try to provide some place of rest for these little ones, he took a house large enough to contain thirty girls.

Rather a remarkable thing happened in connection with the opening of the Home. The money had been supplied, and preparations had been made to receive the children, but none sought admission!

Müller cast about in his mind as to why this should be so, and he discovered that whilst he had asked God for money to open the Home and for helpers, he had forgotten to pray that the children might be sent; and to this he attributed such a strange occurrence.

Still, the omission was soon rectified, and the Home ere long teemed with children.

This was in 1834. From such a small beginning the great Orphan Homes on Ashley Down sprang. Every need connected with the progress of the work was made the subject of prayer by George Müller and his earnest band of workers.

Again and again he has not known where to turn for the next meal for his orphans; but, as if by a miracle, supplies have been *always* forthcoming. Though often in great straits Mr. Müller has never asked for help except of God, and *never* has that help been denied.

The following extract from his journal will show the trials to which Mr. Müller has been subjected: "Never were we so reduced in funds as to-day. There was not a single halfpenny in hand between the matrons of the three orphan houses. There was a good dinner, and by managing to help one another by bread, etc., there was a prospect of getting over the day also; but for none of the houses had we the prospect of being able to take in bread. When I left the brethren and sisters at one o'clock after prayer I told them that we must wait for help, and see how the Lord would deliver us this time." About twenty yards from his home he met a person interested in the Homes who gave him £20. This is but a sample of many occasions upon which, having waited upon God in simple faith, help has arrived at the very hour it has been needed.

Some paragraphs in Müller's yearly reports read almost like a fairy story, only they are far more beautiful, being a record of *facts*. Thus in May, 1892, when the financial year of the institution began, they had in hand for their School, Bible, Missionary and Tract funds only £17 8s. 5-1/2 d.

In June of that year a packet was found at Hereford Railway Station containing eleven sovereigns, addressed to Mr. Müller, with nothing but these words inside, "From a Cheerful Giver, Bristol, for Jesus' Sake". In the same month came £100, "from two servants of the Lord Jesus, who, constrained by the love of Christ, seek to lay up treasure in Heaven".

A Newcastle man wrote that though finances were low he doubled the sum usually sent to the institution, "in faith and also with much joy". A sick missionary in the wilds of Africa sent £44 17s. 5d., being apparently all the money he possessed.

"Again and again," writes Mr. Müller, "I have had cheques amounting even to £5000, from individuals whose names I knew not before receiving their donations."

Other paragraphs in the report read thus: "Received anonymously five large cheeses; received a box of dessert knives and forks, a cruet, a silver soup ladle and a silver cup; from Clifton, twelve tons house coals; from Bedminster, a monster loaf, 200 lbs. in weight, and ten feet long and twenty-one inches broad".

On 1st August £82 5s. came "from a Christian gentleman in Devon, who for more than forty-five years has from time to time helped us, though I have never seen him".

"To-day," writes Müller on 7th September, "our income altogether was about £300 - a plain proof that we do not wait on the Lord in vain; for every donation we receive is a direct answer to prayer, because we never ask a single human being for anything." On 29th October Mr. Müller writes: "For several days very little has come in for the support of the various objects of the institution. To-day, again, only about £15 was received by the first four deliveries of letters; at 5:45 I had for the third time that day prayer with my dear wife, entreating God to help us, and a little after 6 p.m. came a cheque for £200 by the fifth delivery, from Edinburgh."

A gold chain and watch-key, two gold brooches, and a pair of earrings were sent to Mr. Müller, with the following comment: "My wife and I having, through the exceeding riches of God's grace, been brought to the Lord Jesus, wish to lay aside the perishing gold of the world for the unsearchable riches of Christ, and send the enclosed for the support of the orphans".

The above are from a single yearly report - that for 1893. Scores of similar donations in money and kind are recounted in the same annual statement. In that year Mr. Müller was able to speak of his conversion as having taken place nearly sixty-eight years ago. The work has been wonderfully blessed. In the report mentioned Mr. Müller stated that the total amount he had received by prayer and faith for the various objects of his institutions, since 5th March, 1834, had been £1,309,627; that no fewer than 8727 children had been under his care; and that he had room at his Homes for 2050 orphans.

A LABOURER IN THE VINEYARD.

THE STORY OF ROBERT MOFFAT.

"Oh, mother! ask what you will, and I shall do it."

So said Robert Moffat as he stood with his mother on the Firth of Forth waiting for the boat to ferry him across.

He was sixteen years old, and having got a good situation as gardener in Cheshire was bidding farewell that day to home and parents, and about to face the world alone.

His mother had begged him to promise to do whatsoever she asked, and he had hesitated, wishing to know first what it was that she wanted. At last, however, remembering how good and loving she had always been, he had consented. Her request was a very simple one, but it was very far reaching.

"I only ask whether you will read a chapter in the Bible every morning and another every evening."

"Mother," he replied, "you know I read my Bible."

"I know you do," was her answer; "but you do not read it regularly, or as a duty you owe to God, its Author."

"Now I shall return home," she observed when his word had been pledged, "with a happy heart, inasmuch as you have promised to read the Scriptures daily. O Robert, my son, read much in the New Testament! Read much in the Gospels - the blessed Gospels! Then you cannot well go astray. If you pray, the Lord Himself will teach you."

Thus they parted - he starting on his life's journey with her earnest pleadings ringing in his ears.

Travelling in those days (1813) was so slow that it took him a full month to get to High Leigh in Cheshire; and on the way he narrowly escaped being captured by the pressgang and made to serve on a British man-of-war, which was short of hands. The vessel in which he was going south was indeed boarded, and one man seized; but Robert says, "I happened to be in bed, and keep it there as long as they were on deck".

He kept manfully the promise he had made his mother. Notwithstanding the difficulty he experienced in his busy life of setting aside the necessary time for reading two chapters a day from his Bible, he nevertheless faithfully did it.

At first this practice seemed to bring him trouble. It made him feel that he was a sinner, but how to get grace he knew not.

Ere long, however, his fears rolled away. He perceived that being justified by faith he had peace with Christ, and rejoiced in the grace and power of the Lord.

Some good Wesleyans took an interest in the young gardener, and he attended their meetings, which he

F. J. Cross

found very helpful.

When a little later on he was offered a much better situation on the condition that he gave up Methodism he refused it, preferring, as he says, "his God to white and yellow ore".

One day he went to Warrington, and whilst there saw a placard announcing a missionary meeting, at which the Rev. William Roby was to speak. The sight of this reminded him of the descriptions his mother used to read of mission work in Greenland, and the subject became fixed in his mind.

A little later he had the opportunity of hearing Mr. Roby, and determined to call upon him and offer himself for mission work.

So great was his dread of making this call that he asked a companion to accompany him, and be present at the interview, but could only induce his friend to wait for him outside.

When he got to Mr. Roby's door his courage failed him; he looked longingly at his friend and began to retreat. However, his conscience would not allow him to surrender; and back again he went to the house, but still feared to knock.

At length after walking up and down the street in a state of painful indecision he returned and ventured to knock. A terrible moment followed. He would have given anything to run away, and hoped with all his heart Mr. Roby would be out.

This, however, was not the case; and, brought face to

face with the mission preacher, he told his story simply and effectively, and Mr. Roby promised to write to the Missionary Society about him.

At first the offer of his services was declined, but later on it was accepted; and on 30th September, 1816, he was ordained at Surrey Chapel. Amongst others set apart at the same time was John Williams, the martyr of Erromanga.

It was at first proposed that Williams and Moffat should go together to Polynesia; but Mr. Waugh remarked that "thae twa lads were ower young to gang together," so they were separated.

At the age of twenty-one Moffat sailed for South Africa. The ship reached Cape Town, after a voyage of eighty-six days, on 13th January, 1817; and forthwith he started on his career in receipt of a salary of twenty-five pounds per year.

On his journey into the interior he stopped one evening at a Dutch farmer's, where he was warmly welcomed, and was requested to conduct family worship.

Before commencing he asked for the servants. The farmer, roused to indignation by such a request, said he would call in the dogs and baboons if Moffat wanted a congregation of that sort!

But the missionary was not to be denied. In reading the Bible he selected the story of the Syrophoenician woman. Before many minutes had passed the farmer stopped him, saying he would have the servants in.

When the service was over the old man said to Moffat,

"My friend, you took a hard hammer, and you have broken a hard head".

His early missionary efforts were crowned with success. He visited the renowned chief Afrikaner in Namaqualand. This man had given much trouble to the Government, and £100 had been offered for his head. He became, however, sincerely attached to Moffat, and after a time he went to Cape Town with him. The authorities could hardly believe that this notorious robber had become so altered; but right glad were they at the change, and, when Afrikaner returned home, he took with him numerous presents from the Government.

In December, 1819, Moffat was married to Mary Smith at St. George's Church, Cape Town. She had been engaged to him before he left England, and had given up home and parents to go out to Africa and become a missionary's wife. No truer helper could Moffat have found, for she loved the work, and experienced great happiness in her life, notwith-standing all its toils and danger.

Shortly after, Mr. and Mrs. Moffat started for Bechuanaland. They went through many privations, and suffered much from hunger and thirst; but the Gospel was preached to the tribes. Moffat in those days was not only teacher and preacher, but carpenter, smith, cooper, tailor, shoemaker, miller, baker and gardener!

For some years Moffat laboured without seeing much result. One day he said to his wife, "This is hard work, Mary". "It *is* hard work." she replied; "but you must remember the Gospel has never yet been preached to them *in their own tongue*."

Moffat had hitherto taught the natives through an interpreter. He now determined not only to master their language, but to get to know all about their habits and customs, so as to be able to lay hold of them more forcibly. He not only preached the Word in their native tongue, but set up in type and printed the Gospel of St. Luke and some hymns. Then he followed on with the other Gospels and also the Epistles, till the entire of the New Testament was translated into their language.

It must not be thought that a missionary's only cares are those connected with preaching. Far from it. To Mrs. Moffat, who tried to teach the women to be cleanly in their habits, they would say, "Ra Mary, your customs may be good enough for you, but we don't see that they fill the stomach".

The difficulty of getting sufficient food to eat was very real. The soil in the neighbourhood of the station was light and needed plenty of water, but the stream which supplied them with the necessary moisture for their vegetables was diverted from its channel by the natives, so that the missionary's garden was nearly burnt up by the hot sun.

On one occasion Mrs. Moffat asked a native woman to move out of her kitchen, as she wanted to close it before she went to church. For answer the woman hurled a log of wood at her; and she, fearful lest her babe should be hurt, departed, leaving the savage woman in possession of her home.

Whilst Mrs. Moffat had difficulties at home, her husband encountered many dangers abroad. Once whilst going in search of game he came upon a tiger, which seemed as if it were preparing to spring upon him. With the greatest caution he retired slowly from the place, and was just congratulating himself that he was out of danger when he trod on a cobra. The reptile twisted itself about Moffat's leg, and was about to bite him when he managed to level his gun at it and kill it. The poison of this snake is so deadly that had he been bitten his death would have almost instantly followed.

Though he was ready to lay down his life for their good, it was long ere the natives understood how firm a friend he was. At a time of great drought the native "rain-makers" declared that the bell of the chapel frightened away the clouds. So a number of people came to the missionary, and told him they were determined that he must go. But Moffat was not to be awed by the threats of the warriors. He told them that they might kill him, but he should certainly not be driven away. Then the chief and his followers gave up the contest and retired, full of wonder and admiration at his dauntless determination.

Once, whilst Moffat was away on a visit to a neighbouring tribe, his wife was aroused in the night by the report that a hostile tribe had invaded their territory and was close upon them. So Mrs. Moffat had to prepare for flight, but ere she had finished her preparations the good news came that the tribe had gone off in another direction. Yet even then she was in fear for her husband's life. But three weeks later, after enduring terrible anxiety, her husband returned in safety, having managed to escape the enemy.

Gradually a great and wonderful change came over the people amongst whom Robert and Mary Moffat lived.

From utter disregard of teaching they began to exhibit signs of spiritual life, and a number were baptised and received into the Church.

In 1871 Robert and Mary Moffat, after living in Africa for upwards of half a century, returned home. From the letter to Mr. G. Unwin, which is here reproduced in facsimile, it will be seen that Robert Moffat's labours were not even then finished; for up to the last he took the greatest interest in the missionary cause.

His useful life came to an end in August, 1883, when he was in his eighty-eighth year.

F. J. Cross

"THE LADY WITH THE LAMP."

THE STORY OF FLORENCE NIGHTINGALE.

"Lo! in that house of misery
A lady with a lamp I see
Pass through the glimmering gloom,
And flit from room to room."

LONGFELLOW.

"She would speak to one and another, and nod and smile to many more, but she could not do it to all, you know, for we lay there by hundreds; but we could kiss her shadow as it fell, and lay our heads on our pillows again, content."

So wrote one of the soldiers from the hospital at Scutari of Florence Nightingale, the soldier's nurse, and the soldier's friend.

Let us see how it happened that Florence Nightingale was able to do so much for the British soldiers who fought in the Crimea, and why she has left her mark on the history of our times.

Miss Nightingale was born in the city of Florence in the year 1820, and it is from that beautiful Italian town that she derives her Christian name.

Her father was a good and wealthy man, who took great interest in the poor; and her mother was ever seeking to do them some kindness.

Thus Florence saw no little of cottage folk. She took them dainties when they were ailing, and delighted to nurse them when ill.

She loved all dumb animals, and they seemed to know by instinct that she was their friend. One day she came across her father's old shepherd, looking as miserable as could be; and, on inquiring the cause, found that a mischievous boy had thrown a stone at his favourite dog, which had broken its leg, and he was afraid it would have to be killed.

Going together to the shepherd's home they found the dog very excited and angry; but, on Florence speaking to it in her gentle voice, it came and lay down at her feet, and allowed her to examine the damaged limb.

Happily, she discovered it was only bruised; and she attended to it so skilfully that the dog was soon running about in the field again. A few days later she met the shepherd, - he was simply beaming, for the dog had recovered and was with him.

When Florence spoke to the man the dog wagged its tail as much as to say, "I'm mighty glad to see *you* again"; whereupon the shepherd remarked: "Do look at the dog, miss, he be so pleased to hear your voice".

The fact that even her dolls were properly bandaged when their limbs became broken, or the sawdust began to run out of their bodies, will show that even then she was a thoughtful, kindly little person.

When she grew up she wished very much to learn how to nurse the sick.

But in those days it was not considered at all a ladylike thing to do; and, after trying one or two nursing institutions at home, she went to Germany, and afterwards to Paris, in order to make a study of the subject, and to get practical experience in cities abroad.

Miss Nightingale thus learnt nursing very thoroughly, and when she came back to England turned her knowledge to account by taking charge of an institution in London. By good management, tact and skill, the institution became a great success; but she was too forgetful of self, and after a time the hard work told upon her health, and she was obliged to take a rest from her labours.

The time came when the Russian war broke out and Great Britain and France sent their armies into the Crimea. Our men fought like heroes. But it was found out ere many months had passed that those brave fellows, who were laying down their lives for the sake of their country, were being so badly nursed when they were sick and wounded that more were being slain by neglect than by the guns of the enemy.

Then there arose a great cry in Britain; and every one demanded that something should be done to remedy this state of things. But nobody knew quite what to do or how to do it, except one woman, - and that woman was Florence Nightingale.

Mr. Sidney Herbert, the War Minister, was one of the very few people who knew anything about her great powers of organisation; and happily he did know how thoroughly fit she was for the task of properly directing the nursing of the sick soldiers.

So, on the 15th October, 1854, he asked her to go to the Crimea to take entire charge of the nursing arrangements; and in less than a week she started with about forty nurses for Scutari, the town where the great hospital was situated.

All Britain was stirred with admiration at her heroism; for it was well known how difficult was the task she was undertaking. But the quiet gentle woman herself feared neither death, disease nor hard work; the only thing she did not like was the fuss the people made about her.

Scutari, whither she went, is situated on the eastern side of the Bosphorus, opposite Constantinople. Thither the sick and wounded soldiers were being brought by hundreds. It took four or five days to get them from the field of battle to the hospital, their wounds during that tame being generally unattended to. When they arrived at Scutari, it was difficult to land them; after that there was a steep hill up which they had to be carried to the hospital, so that by the time they arrived they were generally in a sad condition. But their trials were not over then. The hospital was dirty and dismal. There was no proper provision for the supply of suitable food, everything was in dire disorder, and the poor fellows died of fever in enormous numbers.

But "the lady with the lamp" soon brought about a

revolution; and the soldiers knew to their joy what it was to have proper nursing. No wonder the men kissed her shadow! Wherever the worst cases were to be found there was Florence Nightingale. Day and night she watched and waited, worked and prayed. Her very presence was medicine and food and light to the soldiers.

Gradually disorder disappeared, and deaths became fewer day by day. Good nursing; care and cleanliness; nourishing food, and - perhaps beyond and above all - love and tenderness, wrought wonders. The oath in the soldier's mouth turned to a prayer at her appearance.

Though the beds extended over a space equal to four miles, yet each man knew that all that human strength could do to forward his recovery was being done.

Before her task was finished Miss Nightingale had taken the fever herself, but her life was mercifully spared.

Since those days, Florence Nightingale has done many kindly and noble deeds. She has always lived as much out of the public sight as possible, though her work has rendered her dear to all hearts.

Though she has had much ill health herself, she has been able to accomplish a splendid life's work, and to advance the study of nursing in all parts of the globe.

FOR ENGLAND, HOME, AND DUTY.

THE DEATH OF NELSON.

It was the 21st October, 1805. The English fleet had been for many days lying off the coast of Spain, eagerly waiting for the navies of France and Spain to leave their shelter in Cadiz harbour. At length, to his joy, Lord Nelson received the signal that they had put out to sea; and he now prepared to attack the combined fleet (which consisted of forty vessels) with his thirty-one ships. Yet, though the enemy not only had more vessels, but they were larger than his own, Nelson confidently expected victory, and told Captain Blackwood he would not be satisfied unless he captured twenty ships. Having made all arrangements, Nelson went down to his cabin and wrote this prayer: -

"May the great God whom I worship grant to my country, and for the benefit of Europe in general, a great and glorious victory; and may no misconduct in any one tarnish it, and may humanity after victory be the predominant feature in the British fleet! For myself individually, I commit my life to Him that made me, and may His blessing alight on my endeavours for serving my country faithfully! To Him I resign myself, and the just cause which is entrusted to me to defend. Amen. Amen. Amen."

F. J. Cross

Before the battle began Nelson made the signal which stirred every heart in the fleet on that day, and has since remained a watchword of the nation: -

"England expects every man will do his duty".

It was received with an outburst of cheering.

Nelson wore, as usual, his admiral's frock-coat. On his breast glittered four stars of the different orders which had been given him. He was in good spirits, and eager for the fray.

His officers represented to him how desirable it was that he should keep out of the battle as long as possible; and, knowing the truth of this, he signalled to the other ships to go in front. Yet his desire to be in the forefront of the attack was so great that he would not take in any sail on The Victory, and thus rendered it impossible for the other vessels to obey his orders.

At ten minutes to twelve the battle began; by four minutes past twelve fifty men on board Nelson's ship *The Victory* had been killed or wounded, and many of her sails shot away.

The fire of the enemy was so heavy that Nelson, smiling, said, "This is too warm work, Hardy, to last long". Up to that time not a shot had been fired from *The Victory*; and Nelson declared that never in all his battles had he seen anything which surpassed the cool courage of his crew. Then, however, when they had come to close quarters with the enemy, from both sides of *The Victory* flashed forth the fire of the guns, carrying swift destruction among the foe.

The French ship next which they were lying, *The Redoutable*, having ceased firing her great guns, Nelson twice gave instructions to stop firing into her, with the humane desire of avoiding unnecessary slaughter. Strange to say, that from this ship at a quarter past one was fired a shot which struck him in the left shoulder, and proved fatal.

Within twenty minutes after the fatal shot had been fired from *The Redoutable* that ship was captured, the man who killed Nelson having himself been shot by a midshipman on board *The Victory*.

When he had been taken down to the cockpit he insisted that the surgeon should leave him and attend to others; "for," said he, "you can do nothing for me".

At this time his sufferings were very great, but he was cheered by the news which they brought him from time to time. At half-past two Hardy could report "ten ships have struck". An hour later he came with the news that fourteen or fifteen had struck. "That's well," cried Nelson, "but I bargained for twenty."

A little later he said, "Kiss me, Hardy". Hardy knelt down, and Nelson said, "Now I am satisfied. Thank God I have done my duty". After that it became difficult for him to speak, but he several times repeated the words, "Thank God I have done my duty". And these were the last words he uttered before he died. At half-past four o'clock he expired.

Thus Nelson died in the hour of victory. He had won a battle which once and for all broke the naval power of France and Spain, and delivered Great Britain from all fear of attack by the great Napoleon.

F. J. Cross

A WOMAN WHO SUCCEEDED BY FAILURE.

THE STORY OF HARRIET NEWELL.

This is rather an exceptional chapter: for it tells of a very little life judged by length of days, a very sad life judged by some of its incidents, a very futile life considered by what it actually accomplished, - but a very wonderful life regarded in the light of the results which followed.

Harriet Attwood was born in Massachusetts, America, in the year 1793.

Even in her girlhood she looked forward to assisting in making the Gospel known in distant lands. Long before any movement sprang up in America for sending out female missionaries to the heathen, the day dream of this little girl was to devote herself to the mission cause.

Not that she dreamed away her life in longing, and neglected her every-day duties. She was remarkable for her intelligence and dutiful conduct; and from the age of ten felt deep religious convictions, and was constant in her daily prayers and Bible reading.

Her life was brightened by her belief, and she ever kept in view what she believed to be her mission in life.

"What can I do," she writes, "that the light of the Gospel may shine upon the heathen? They are perishing for lack of knowledge, while I enjoy the glorious privileges of a Christian land."

The means of accomplishing her desire soon came. A young missionary, named Newell, who was going out to India, asked her to become his wife.

Her decision was not taken without earnest prayer; and had her parents opposed her wishes she would have been prepared to give them up, but, gaining their consent, she accepted Mr. Newell's offer. She was fully aware that the difficulties in the way would be very great; for up to that time no female missionary had gone from America to the mission field.

At first her friends tried in every way to dissuade her from leaving home, and, as they termed it, "throwing herself away on the heathen".

But her simplicity of belief and earnestness of purpose soon changed their thoughts on the subject and when, early in the year 1812, Mr. and Mrs. Newell sailed for Calcutta, many came together to wish them God-speed on their perilous journey.

On his arrival in Calcutta Mr. Newell, in accordance with the regulation of the East India Company at that time, reported himself at the police office; and to his sorrow found that the Company would not allow any missionaries to work in their dominions!

Here was a disappointing beginning for these earnest young people! At first it seemed quite probable they would not even be allowed to land; and though permission was after a time obtained, yet in six weeks they were told they must go elsewhere, as they would not be permitted to settle.

A few days later, however, the prospect brightened. "We have obtained leave," writes Mrs. Newell, "to go to the Isle of France (Mauritius). We hear that the English Governor there favours missions; that a large field of usefulness is there opened - 18,000 inhabitants ignorant of Jesus. Is not this the station that Providence has designed for us? A door is open wide. Shall we not enter and help the glorious work?"

But it was by her influence alone that she was permitted to engage in the work her heart longed for. On the journey to Mauritius rapid consumption set in, and day by day she became weaker.

Although she felt at first a natural disappointment that she would not be allowed to labour in the mission field, she was able to look upward in her hour of trial and to say: "Tell my friends I never regretted leaving my native land for the cause of Christ. God has called me away before we have entered on the work of the mission, but the case of David affords me comfort. I have it in my heart to do what I can for the heathen, and I hope God will accept me."

On the 30th November, 1812, at the early age of nineteen, Harriet Newell passed away.

Might not many a one justly ask, was not her life a failure? And the answer, based on the experience and results of what her life and death accomplished, is No - emphatically No!

For her example produced a wave of religious life and missionary enthusiasm in America, the like of which has hardly ever been known.

The very fact of this whole-hearted girl giving up her life for the cause of Christ, and the pathos of her untimely end, did more to touch the hearts of multitudes than perhaps the most apparently successful accomplishment of her mission would have done.

A MARTYR OF THE SOUTH SEAS.

THE MORNING AND EVENING OF BISHOP PATTESON'S LIFE.

John Coleridge Patteson was born in April, 1827. He was blessed with an upright and good father, and a loving and gentle mother; and thus his early training was calculated to make him the earnest Christian man he afterwards became.

Here is an extract from a letter written from school at the age of nine, which shows that he had faults and failings to overcome just like all other boys: -

"My dear papa, I am very sorry for having told so many falsehoods, which Uncle Frank has told mama of. I am very sorry for having done so many bad things - I mean falsehoods - and I heartily beg your pardon; and Uncle Frank says that he thinks if I stay, in a month's time Mr. Cornish will be able to trust me again.... He told me that if I ever told another falsehood he should that instant march me into the school and ask Mr. Cornish to strip and birch me ... but I will not catch the birching."

And he did not. He was so frank, so ready to see his own faults, that he was always a favourite. Uncle Frank remarked of him at this same time: "He wins one's heart in a moment".

Perhaps one ought to call him a Queen's missionary, for her Majesty saved him from a serious accident in a rather remarkable manner.

In 1838 when the Queen was driving in her carriage the crowd was so dense that Patteson, then at school at Eton, became entangled in the wheel of the carriage and would have been thrown underneath and run over had it not been for the young Queen's quick perception. Seeing the danger she gave her hand to the boy, who readily seized it, and was thus able to get on his feet again and avoid the threatened peril.

He was a boy who, when he had done wrong, always blamed himself - not any one else. Thus, when he was twelve, having spent a good deal of his time one term at Eton enjoying cricket and boating, he found his tutor was not at all satisfied with his progress. "I am ashamed to say," he remarked in writing home, "that I can offer not the slightest excuse: my conduct on this occasion has been very bad. I expect a severe reproof from you, and pray do not send me any money. But from this time I am determined I will not lose a moment."

In 1841 came the first indication of what his future career might be.

Bishop Selwyn of New Zealand was preaching, and the boy says of the sermon: "It was beautiful when he talked of his going out to found a church, and then to die neglected and forgotten".

How deep had been the influence on his mind of his

mother's example may be gathered from the letter he wrote at the time of her death in 1842, when he was fifteen years old: "It is a very dreadful loss for us all, but we have been taught by that dear mother who has now been taken from us that it is not fit to grieve for those who die in the Lord, 'for they rest from their labours'.... She said once, 'I wonder I wish to leave you, my dearest John, and the children and this sweet place, but yet I do wish it'; so lovely was her faith."

In 1854 Bishop Selwyn returned to England. During the time that had elapsed since his previous visit, Patteson had been ordained. The bishop stayed with his father a few days, and during that time the feelings which the boy of fourteen had experienced were revived in the man of twenty-seven; and with his father's consent John Coleridge Patteson entered upon his life work, sailing with Bishop Selwyn for the South Seas in March, 1855.

There he laboured with such energy and success that in 1861 he was consecrated bishop. Many thousands of miles were traversed by him in the mission ship *The Southern Cross*, visiting the numerous islands of the Pacific known as Polynesia or Melanesia.

Of the dangers that abounded he knew ample to try his courage. On arriving at Erromanga (the scene of Williams' martyrdom) on one occasion he found that Mr. Gordon, the missionary, and his wife had recently both been treacherously slain by the natives. At another island, as he returned to the boat, he saw one of the natives draw a bow with the apparent intention of shooting him, and then unbend it at the entreaty of his comrades. "But," remarks the bishop in recording this, "we must try to effect more frequent landings."

And thus full of faith he laboured on, telling the people of these scattered islands, which besprinkle the southern ocean like stars in the milky way, of the love of Christ.

He was still ready to condemn himself just as he did in his early days. From Norfolk Island, in 1870, he wrote to his sister when he was holding an ordination: "At such times as these, when one is specially engaged in solemn work, there is much heart searching; and I cannot tell you how my conscience accuses me of such systematic selfishness during many long years - I mean I see how I was all along making self the centre, and neglecting all kinds of duties - social and others - in consequence".

He was much grieved by the accounts which reached him of the terrible war which was being fought between France and Germany in 1870. "What can I say," he writes, "to my Melanesians about it? Do these nations believe in the gospel of peace and goodwill? Is the sermon on the mount a reality or not?"

Yet he had troubles closer at home than this even. The trading ships were coming in numbers to the islands, and carrying off the natives either by guile or by force to Fiji and other places where labourers were wanted.

Notwithstanding the anxieties which beset him on this account, the good bishop continued to work as hard as ever, and very happy he was about his people.

On Christmas Eve, 1870, he writes: "Seven new communicants to-morrow morning. And all things, God be praised, happy and peaceful about us." He wrote of the large "family" of 145 Melanesian natives he had around him; at another time he spoke of his sleeping on a table with some twelve or more fellows about him; and people coming and going all day long both in and out of school hours!

In August, 1871, he baptised 248 persons, twenty-five of them adults, all in a little more than a month, and he rejoiced in the thought that a blessed change was going on in the hearts of these people.

He had never experienced such cheering success before, and, though his friends were endeavouring to persuade him to take rest and change for his health's sake, he determined to labour on while there was so much need for his exertion and such blessed results followed.

The desire to believe on the part of some of his people was very touching. One of them said to him: "I don't know how to pray properly, but I and my wife say, 'God make our hearts light - take away the darkness. We believe that You love us because You sent Jesus to become a man and die for us; but we can't understand it all. Make us fit to be baptised.'"

Some, of course, were not so enlightened as that. After the kidnapping traders had been harrying the islands, one of the chiefs said that, if the bishop would only bring a man-of-war and get him vengeance on his adversaries, he would be exalted like his Father above.

There was indeed serious cause for the anger of the natives. One of them related how he had been out to a vessel with his companions, and a white man had come down into the canoe and presently upset it, seizing him by the belt. Happily this broke, and he swam under the side of the canoe and finally got on shore, but the other three were killed - their heads were cut off and taken on board, and their bodies thrown to the sharks. The assailants were men-stealers, who killed ruthlessly that they might present heads to the chiefs.

Five natives from the same island were also killed or carried off, and thus when the bishop visited them they were in a state of sullen wrath.

On the 20th of September, 1871, Bishop Patteson came to Nukapu. The island is difficult of approach at low water, and the little ship, *The Southern Cross*, could not get close in. So the bishop went off to the shore in a boat and got into one of the canoes, leaving his four pupils to await his return. They saw him land, and he was then lost to sight.

About half an hour later the natives in the canoes, without the least warning, began shooting their arrows at the poor fellows in the boat, and ere it could be taken out of bowshot one of them was pierced with six arrows, and two of the others were also wounded.

They were full of fears about the bishop, and, notwithstanding the danger, determined to seek for him. They had no arms except one pistol which the mate possessed.

As they made their way towards shore a canoe drifted out, and lying in it, wrapped in a native mat, was the body of Bishop Patteson.

A sweet calm smile was on his face, a palm leaf was fastened upon his breast, and upon the body were five wounds - the exact number of the natives who had been kidnapped or killed.

So the good bishop died for the misdeeds of others. The natives but followed their traditions in exacting blood for blood, and their poor dark minds could not distinguish between the good and the bad white men.

Two of those who were with the bishop in the boat, and had received arrow wounds, died within a week, after much suffering.

One of them, Mr. Atkins, writing of the occurrence on the day of the martyrdom, says: -

"It would be selfish to wish him back. He has gone to his rest, dying, as he lived, in the Master's service. It seems a shocking way to die; but I can say from experience it is far more to hear of than to suffer. There is no sign of fear or pain on his face, just the look that he used to have when asleep, patient and a little wearied. What his mission will do without him, God only knows who has taken him away."

Three days after, in celebrating the Holy Communion, Mr. Atkins stumbled in his speech, and then he and his companions knew the poison in his system was working. "Stephen and I," he said, "are going to follow the bishop. Don't grieve about it ... It is very good because God would have it so, because He only looks after us, and He understands about us, and now He wills to take us too and *it is well*."

"K.G. AND COSTER."

SOME ANECDOTES ABOUT LORD SHAFTESBURY.

"And where shall we write to?" asked one of the costermongers.

"Address your letter to me at Grosvenor Square," replied Lord Shaftesbury, "and it will probably reach me; but, if after my name you put 'K.G. and Coster,' there will be no doubt that I shall get it!"

This conversation took place at the conclusion of a meeting which had been held by the costermongers. They had met to talk about their grievances, and Lord Shaftesbury had attended the gathering and promised to help them, telling them to write to him if they required further assistance.

The noble Knight of the Garter was not only interested in the costermongers themselves, but in their animals too.

At one time the costers had used their donkeys and ponies shamefully, had overworked and underfed them; but gradually they were made to see how much better it was to treat their animals well. With a good Sunday rest and proper treatment, the donkeys would go thirty miles a day comfortably; without it, they could not do more than half.

So, as Lord Shaftesbury had been kind to the costers and taken such interest in their pursuits, they invited him to a special meeting, at which they presented him with a splendid donkey.

Over a thousand costers with their friends were there, when the donkey, profusely decorated with ribbons, was led to the platform. Lord Shaftesbury vacated the chair and made way for the new arrival; and then, putting his arm round the animal's neck, returned thanks in a short speech in which he said: -

"When I have passed away from this life I desire to have no more said of me than that I have done my duty, as the poor donkey has done his - with patience and unmurmuring resignation".

The donkey was then led down the steps of the platform, and Lord Shaftesbury remarked, "I hope the reporters of the press will state that, the donkey having vacated the chair, the place was taken by Lord Shaftesbury".

Let us turn for a moment to the beginning of his life, and see how it was that Lord Shaftesbury was induced to devote himself so heartily to the good of the poor and oppressed.

Maria Mills, his old nurse, had not a little to do with this. She was one of those simple-minded humble Christians who, all unknowingly, plant in many minds the good seed which grows up and brings forth much fruit.

She was very fond of the little boy, and would tell him the "sweet story of old" in so attractive a manner that a deep impression was made upon his heart. The prayers she taught him in childhood he not only used in his youth, but even in old age the words were often upon his lips.

When he was a schoolboy at Harrow came the turning point in his life.

He saw four or five drunken men carrying a coffin containing the remains of a companion; and such was their state of intoxication that they dropped it, and then broke out into foul language.

The effect this had upon the youth was so great that he resolved to devote his life to helping the poor and friendless.

There was plenty of work for him to do. Children in factories and mines required to be protected from the cruelties to which they were subjected; chimney sweeps needed to be guarded from the dangers to which they were exposed; the hours of labour in factories were excessive; thieves required to be shown a way of escape from their wretched life; ragged schools and other institutions needed support.

These and numerous other matters kept Lord Shaftesbury hard at work during the entire of his long life, and by his help many wise alterations were made in the laws of the country.

"Do what is right and trust to Providence for the rest," was his motto; and he stuck to it always.

Lord Shaftesbury brought before Parliament a scheme for assisting young thieves to emigrate; and the grown-up burglars and vagabonds, seeing how much in earnest he was, invited him to a meeting. To this he went without a moment's hesitation.

The door was guarded by a detachment of thieves, who watched to see that none but those of their class went in.

Lord Shaftesbury was in the chair, and the meeting commenced with prayer. There were present over two hundred burglars and criminals of the worst kind, besides a great number of other bad characters.

First of all the chairman gave an address; then some of the thieves followed, telling quite plainly and simply how they spent their lives.

When Lord Shaftesbury urged them to give up their old lives of sin one of them said, "We must steal or we shall die".

The city missionary, who was present, urged them to pray, as God could help them.

"But," said one of the men, "my Lord and gentlemen of the jury (!), prayer is very good, but it won't fill an empty stomach."

It was, indeed, a difficult problem how best to aid the poor fellows; but Lord Shaftesbury solved it. As a result of the conference three hundred thieves went abroad to Canada to begin life anew, or were put into the way of earning an honest living.

One of the subjects which occupied a great deal of Lord Shaftesbury's attention was the condition of the young in coal mines and factories.

At that date children began to work in mines at the age of four or five, and large numbers of girls and boys were labouring in the pits by the time they were eight. For twelve or fourteen hours a day these poor little toilers had to sit in the mines, opening and shutting trap doors as the coal was pushed along in barrows. All alone, with no one to speak to, sitting in a damp, stifling atmosphere, the poor children had to stay day after day; and if they went to sleep they got well beaten. Rats and mice were their only companions, and Sunday was the only day on which they were gladdened by the daylight.

It was a shocking state of existence, nor did it grow better as the children got older.

Then they had to drag heavy loads along the floors of the mine. When the passages were narrow the boys and girls had a girdle fastened round their waists, a chain was fixed to this, and passed between their legs and hooked to the carriage. Then, crawling on hands and knees through the filth and mire, they pulled these trucks as cattle would drag them, whilst their backs were bruised and wounded by knocking against the low roof.

Girls and women were made to carry heavy weights of coal. Children stood ankle deep in water, pumping hour after hour, and their work was sometimes prolonged for thirty-six hours continuously; so that it was no wonder the children died early, that they suffered much from disease, and led cheerless, wretched lives.

Against such cruelties Lord Shaftesbury was constantly warring; and his warfare was not in vain.

Quite as badly off were the little chimney sweeps. Boys were kidnapped, and sold to cruel masters, who forced them to climb high chimneys filled with soot and smoke. If they refused, a fire was perhaps lighted below, and they would thus be forced to ascend. The consequence was that many terrible accidents happened, resulting in the deaths of these poor little fellows, whilst numbers died early from disease.

Lord Shaftesbury roused the country to a sense of the wrong that was being done to the chimney sweeps, and Bills were passed in Parliament for their protection.

Not only children, but men and women also, needed to be defended from wrong and overwork.

Lord Shaftesbury visited the factories to see how the labourers were actually treated; and this is one of the things that came under his notice.

A young woman whilst working in a mill at Stockport was caught by the machinery and badly injured. When the accident happened she had not completed her week's work, so eighteenpence was deducted from her wages!

Horrified at such treatment Lord Shaftesbury brought an action against the owners of the factory, and obtained £100 for the woman.

For shorter hours and better treatment of factory hands the earl struggled in and out of Parliament; and, though the battle was long and fierce, it ended in victory.

Such labour took up much time, and brought many expenses to the good earl. It brought him, too, plenty of enemies; for most of his life was devoted to striving to make the rich and selfish do justice to the poor and downcast.

He not only gave his time, but his money too; and oftentimes, though the eldest son of an earl, and later an earl himself, he hardly knew where to turn for the means to keep his schemes going.

One day a lady called on him, and, telling a piteous tale of a Polish refugee, asked him for help. Lord Shaftesbury had to confess he had no money he could give; then he suddenly remembered he had five pounds in the library: he fetched the bank note, which formed his nest egg, and presented it to her.

One of Lord Shaftesbury's greatest works was the promotion of ragged schools.

To these schools, established in the poorest neighbourhoods of the metropolis, came the street arabs, the poor and abandoned, and received kindness and teaching, which comforted and civilised them. The outcasts who slept in doorways, under arches, and in all kinds of horrible and unhealthy places, were the objects of this good man's care; and ways were found of benefiting and starting afresh hundreds of lads who would otherwise have become thieves or vagabonds in the great city.

When he was over eighty years old he was still striving for the good of others. So much was his heart in the work that he remarked on one occasion: "When I feel age creeping on me, and know I must soon die - I hope it is not wrong to say it - but I cannot bear to leave the world with all the misery in it".

The dawn came for him in October, 1885, when in his eighty-fifth year this veteran leader was called to his rest.

For convenience I have spoken of him throughout as Lord Shaftesbury; but it may be well to mention that till he was fifty years old he was known as Lord Ashley. Through the death of his father he became Earl of Shaftesbury in 1851.

A STATESMAN WHO HAD NO ENEMIES.

THE STORY OF W.H. SMITH.

It is always well to remember that the man who serves his country as a good citizen, as a soldier, as a statesman, or in any other walk of life, deserves our admiration as much as the missionary or the minister of the Gospel - each and all such are servants of the great King.

By far the greater portion of our lives is spent at the desk or the counter, in the office, shop, or field; so that it is of the first importance we should keep the strictest watch on our actions in our work as well as in our leisure moments.

One of the most successful men in commerce and politics of the century was Mr. W.H. Smith. Strange to say, the desires of his early days were entirely opposed to business life. At the age of sixteen he greatly desired to proceed to one of the universities, and prepare for becoming a clergyman, but his parents being opposed to such a step he gave up the idea in deference to their wishes.

It was a great disappointment to him to do this - yet he was able to write, "It is my duty to acknowledge an overruling and directing Providence in all the very

F. J. Cross

minutest things, by being in whatever state I am therewith content. My conclusion is, then, that I am at present pursuing the path of duty, however imperfectly; wherever it may lead, or what it may become, I know not."

Thus did William Henry Smith see the door of the Church closed upon him with no vain regrets, but in a spirit of submission to his father's wishes. Writing of these days many years later, when as a Minister of the Crown he was in attendance upon her Majesty at Balmoral, he says: "I thought my life was aimless, purposeless, and I wanted something else to do; but events compelled me to what promised to be a dull life and a useless one: the result is that few men have had more interesting work to do".

In his earlier years W.H. Smith made a list of subjects for daily prayer, embracing repentance, faith, love, grace to help, gratitude, power to pray, constant direction in all things, a right understanding of the Bible, deliverance from besetting sin, constancy in God's service, relatives and friends, missionaries, pardon for all ignorance and sin in prayer, etc., etc.; and it was one of the characteristics of his nature that he felt prayer both in youth and age to be *a necessity*.

It was a busy life in which Smith was launched at the commencement of his career.

His father had already laid the foundation of the newsagency business which is now of world-wide fame. Every week-day morning, summer and winter, throughout the year, sunshine or rain, fog or snow, father and son left their home for the business house in the Strand, at four o'clock. Sometimes, indeed, the younger man was at his post as early as three o'clock in the morning; and from the time he arrived at the place of business there was constant work to be done. It was difficult and anxious work too, and the constant strain told upon the young man's health.

The collection and distribution of newspapers, which formed then the chief part of the business of W.H. Smith & Son, was one that needed the closest attention and the most untiring energy.

"First on the road" was old Mr. Smith's motto; and he carried it out.

Smith's carts were in attendance at all the great newspaper offices, ready to carry off printed sheets to the Strand house for sorting and packing; and thence they sped swiftly through the streets in the early morning to catch the first trains for the country. Occasionally *The Times*, which was the last printed journal, did not arrive at the station till the final moment. The whistle would have sounded, the doors would have all been locked, the guard would have given his warning signal, when in would come at hurricane speed Smith's cart bearing its load of "Thunderers". Ready hands would seize the papers, and the last packet would perchance be thrown in as the train was already steaming out of the station.

A great deal of the forwarding of newspapers was in those days done by coaches. To catch these with the later papers, Smith had light carts with fast horses. If the coaches had started, Smith's carts would pursue for many miles, till they caught up the coaches at one of their stopping places.

At the death of William IV. Smith made gigantic efforts to distribute the papers early, and he got them into the country many hours before the ordinary mails would have taken them. He even hired a special ship to carry over the papers to Ireland, so that they reached Belfast on the same day. By such means the fame of Smith grew rapidly, and the business vastly increased. When Mr. W.H. Smith became a partner in 1846, at the age of twenty-one, it was valued at over £80,000.

But wear and tear and the anxieties of business life had made old Mr. Smith often quick-tempered, and difficult to please; and the coming of Mr. "W.H." into the business was hailed with pleasure by the workmen: he was so full of tact and sympathy; and sometimes, when his father had raised a storm of ill-feeling by some hasty expressions, he was able to bring peace and calm by his pleasant and genial manner.

Yet he was every inch a man of business, and even more clear-headed and far-seeing than the senior partner, his father.

It was he who commenced the railway bookstall business.

Every one knows the familiar look of Smith's bookstalls, with their energetic clerks, and their armies of pushing newsboys, and perchance think they were born with the railways and have grown up with them.

But such is not the case. It was not till about 1850 that Mr. W.H. Smith secured the entire bookstall rights on the London and North-Western Railway, much against his father's advice. The vast improvement in the selection of books and the service of papers, however, induced other companies to desire to have a similar arrangement, till the chief portion of all the English railways came to be girdled by Smith's bookstalls.

From this date the business advanced with giant strides. Managers and clerks had to be engaged, the latter in large numbers. Here the genius of Smith as a judge of character was abundantly shown. He came to a determination almost at a glance, and seldom erred in his judgment.

In 1868 he was returned to Parliament, and in 1874 Mr. Disraeli selected him for a place in his Ministry. A year later he was made First Lord of the Admiralty. How serviceable he had been in the former post may be judged by the remark made by Sir Stafford Northcote when he lost Smith's assistance on his promotion to the higher position: "I am troubled to know what to do without my right hand. I don't think he made a slip in the whole three years."

Writing to his wife when he was appointed First Lord of the Admiralty, Mr. Smith says: "My patent has come to-day, and I have taken my seat at the Board, who address me as 'Sir' in every sentence. It is strange, and makes me shy at first; and I have to do what I hardly like - to send for them, not to go to them; but I am told they expect me, as their chief, to require respect."

He often wrote to his wife whilst the debates were going on in the House of Commons. "Here I am, sitting listening to Arthur Balfour, who is answering Mr. J. Morley," he writes; "and I have ears for him and thoughts for my dear ones at home."

"Remember me in your prayers" is a request he often makes to his wife and children. In 1886 the Rt. Hon. W. H. Smith became leader of the House of Commons, and had thus reached one of the highest positions any Englishman can occupy. "Old Morality" was the nickname by which he was known; and this term is one of great honour. No man ever gained higher respect from all parties, and no man was ever more fully trusted by the people at large. Thus though Mr. Smith never entered the Church, and perchance missed a bishopric, yet he was a good citizen of the world and a humble Christian, devoting his best energies to the service of his Queen and country.

"GREATER THAN AN ARCHBISHOP."

ANECDOTES ABOUT THE REV. CHARLES SIMEON.

"As to Simeon," wrote Macaulay, "if you knew what his authority and influence were, and how they extended from Cambridge to the most remote corners of England, you would allow that his real sway over the Church was far greater than that of any primate."

There is little recorded of Simeon's early life to indicate the character of the future leader of men; for, to "jump over half a dozen chairs in succession, and snuff a candle with his feet," is an ordinary schoolboy accomplishment. Yet there is one incident which shows he could be in earnest in religious matters, even at that date.

Whilst he was at Eton, in 1776, a national fast-day was appointed on account of the war with America, which was then in progress. Simeon, feeling that, if any one had displeased God more than others, it was certainly he, spent the day in prayer and fasting. So great was the ridicule, however, which followed, that he gave up his serious thoughts for the time, though it is related that he kept an alms-box, into which he put money whenever his conscience accused him of wrong-doing.

F. J. Cross

It was rather a favourite habit of his to punish himself by fines for bad behaviour. Later on in life, when he found it difficult to rise early in the morning, he resolved to give the servant half a crown every time he played the part of the sluggard. One morning he found himself reasoning in his own mind, whilst enjoying a warm, comfortable bed, that, after all, half-crowns were very acceptable to the poor woman who received them. But he made up his mind to put an end, once and for all, to such suggestions from the tempter; and resolved accordingly that, if he got up late again, he would throw a guinea into the Cam. He did it too. The next time he rose late he walked down to the river, and threw a hard-earned guinea into the water. It was worth while, nevertheless; for he never had to punish himself again for the same fault.

The turning point in his life came soon after his arrival at Cambridge.

The provost sent him a message to say that he would be required to partake of the Holy Communion at mid-term, then about three weeks distant.

The thought of so solemn an occasion weighed heavily on his mind. He at once set about reading devotional manuals, and sorrowed earnestly for his past sins. So heavy, indeed, lay the burden of sin upon him that he envied the very dogs, wishing that he could change places with them.

For three months this state of feeling continued. But in Passion Week the thought came to him that God had provided an Offering for him, on whose head he could lay his sins, just as the Jewish high priest laid the sins of the people on the head of the scapegoat. He saw dimly at first that his sins could be, and were intended to be, transferred to Christ; and he determined to lay them upon the Saviour, and be rid of them.

On Wednesday hope dawned in his heart; on Thursday it increased; on Friday and Saturday it grew and developed; and on Easter Day, 1778, he awoke with the words on his lips: -

"Jesus Christ is risen to-day, Hallelujah!" and, better still, written once and for ever in his heart.

In his twentieth year he had experienced that deep conviction known as conversion.

Like every true convert, Simeon, having found the way himself, now endeavoured to help others to realise the same blessed hope.

His intimate friends were told of the new joy that had come to him: he instructed the women who worked at the colleges, and when he went home induced his relatives to commence family prayers.

Though the light had dawned upon him he was nevertheless full of faults. He dressed showily, went to races, spent his Sundays carelessly.

But gradually these habits were overcome, and he grew in holiness, becoming watchful of his conduct, praying more fervently, living nearer to Christ.

In 1782 Simeon was ordained deacon in Ely Cathedral, and shortly after became honorary curate to Mr. Atkinson, vicar of St. Edward's Church, near King's College. He was already a marked man on account of his earnest life. He visited the parishioners as Mr. Atkinson's substitute, and was soon received with pleasure by them.

The church became so full that the people could hardly find room. It is related that even the clerk's desk was invaded, and that when Mr. Atkinson returned after a holiday the clerk met him with the following strange welcome: -

"Oh, sir, I am so glad you are come: Now we shall have some room!"

On the very first Sunday he took duty he showed the metal of which he was made; for, in going home after service, he heard voices high in dispute in one of the houses he passed. Straightway he went in, reproved the couple who were at strife, and knelt down to pray. Peace was restored, and Simeon's character for earnestness was confirmed.

Now came an eventful period in this good man's life. The minister of Trinity Church, Cambridge, having died, Simeon was appointed by the bishop.

The parishioners, however, desired to have as minister the curate; and, as it was impossible to gratify their wish, they made matters as unpleasant as possible for Simeon.

The pew doors were nearly all kept locked, so that the space left for the congregation was much reduced.

On the first Sunday there was practically no congregation; but later on people could not resist his influence, and the church began to fill. To provide places for those who came, Simeon had seats placed in various parts of the building. The churchwardens, however, threw them out into the church-yard!

It was an uncomfortable beginning; but Simeon persevered. He began a course of Sunday evening lectures, to which the people flocked in crowds; but the churchwardens locked the church doors and carried off the keys.

Besides beings rude and unmannerly, that was distinctly illegal; but Simeon put up with the affront for the sake of peace.

When necessary he could be firm. The young men threw stones at the church windows and broke them. On one occasion Simeon discovered the offender, and obliged him to read a public confession of his fault.

The church was crowded. The young man read the paper which Simeon had prepared for him, but did so in a voice low and partially inaudible. Then Simeon himself, taking the paper from him, read the apology in such tones that none could fail to hear.

The young men were impressed, and the congregation listened to the sermon that followed with more than usual attention.

He was of all men the most humble; yet this did not prevent his speaking honestly and openly when he considered by so doing he could be of service. Thus a friend once asked him, after having preached a showy sermon with which he himself was remarkably satisfied, "How did I speak this evening?"

"Why, my dear brother," said Simeon, "I am sure you will pardon me; you know it is all love, my brother - but, indeed, it was just as if you were knocking on a warming-pan - tin, tin, tin, tin, without any intermission!"

Once a party of undergraduates laid an ambush for Simeon, intending to assault him. He, however, by accident happened to go home that night another way.

Not only had he to put up with active but also with much passive opposition. But he went on in faith and charity, till his enemies became his friends - his friends, his ardent and reverent admirers.

We must pass over without further comment a life of humility, love, and holiness - a life full of good works at home, and ardently interested in missions abroad.

In 1831, when Simeon was seventy-two years old, he preached his last sermon before the university. The place was crowded. The heads of houses, the doctors, the masters of art, the bachelors, the undergraduates, the townsmen, all crowded to hear the venerable preacher. They hung on his words and listened with the deepest reverence.

His closing days were singularly bright and happy. Three weeks before his death a friend, seeing him look more than usually calm and peaceful, asked him what he was thinking of.

"I don't think now," he answered brightly; "I enjoy."

At another time his friends, believing the end was at hand, gathered round him.

"You want to see," he remarked, "what is called a dying scene. That I abhor.... I wish to be alone with my God, the lowest of the low."

One evening those watching beside him thought he was unconscious, his eyes having been closed for some hours. But suddenly he remarked: -

"If you want to know what I am doing, go and look in the first chapter of Ephesians from the third to the fourteenth verse; there you will see what I am enjoying now."

On Sunday, 13th November, just as the bells of St. Mary's were calling together the worshippers to service he passed away. He had accepted an invitation to preach a course of four sermons, and would have delivered the second of the course on that very afternoon. I am permitted, by the kindness of the Rev. H.C.G. Moule, from whose delightful biography the foregoing sketch has been compiled, to reproduce a page from this address.

"Who would ever have thought I should behold such a day as this?" wrote Simeon. "My parish sweetly harmonious, my whole works stereotyping in twenty-one volumes, and my ministry not altogether inefficient at the age of seventy-three.... But I love the valley of humiliation."

In that last sentence, perhaps, lies the secret of the man's far-reaching and undying influence.

A SOLDIER MISSIONARY.

THE STORY OF HEDLEY VICARS.

It was the 22nd March, 1855, just outside Sebastopol. The night was dark and gusty. Close to the Russian entrenchments was an advanced post of the British forces, commanded by Captain Hedley Vicars. Fifteen thousand Russians under cover of the gloom had come out from Sebastopol and driven our French allies out of their advanced trenches. Then a portion of this force stealthily advanced, seeking to take the British by surprise.

The first to discover the presence of the enemy was Hedley Vicars. With great judgment he made his men lie down till the Russians were within twenty paces. Then, springing to his feet, he shouted: -

"Now, 97th, on your pins and charge!"

His force was about 200, that of the enemy nearly 2000! Wounded in the breast at the first onset, he still led the charge. "Men of the 97th, follow me!" rang out his voice above the din of battle, and leaping the parapet of the entrenchment he charged the enemy down the ravine. "This way, 97th!" was his last command - still at the head of his men. His sword had already dealt with two of the foe, and was again uplifted, when a musket shot, fired at close quarters, severed an artery; and the work on earth of this gallant man was over.

Hedley Vicars was a true soldier and earnest Christian. The last words he wrote, penned the night before he died, were: "I spent the evening with Cay. I read Isaiah, xli.; and he prayed. We walked together during the day, and exchanged our thoughts about Jesus."

He spent a busy time in the Crimea, doing plenty of hard work in the trenches; and when off duty engaged in hospital visiting, tract and book distributing, attending prayer meetings and mission services, constant in his Bible reading, and always endeavouring to do good to others.

Here is an entry from his diary on the 4th March, 1855: "Sunday. Had Divine service in camp. We afterwards met together in a tent. All present. Then sat on a regimental board, after which I went to the Guards' camp for Cay; and we then went, laden with tracts, books and prayers, to the remaining hospitals of the Second Division, where we distributed all we had. Had service in our hospital tent on my return, and prayed with one of the sick, particularly, who asked me to do so... I spoke to him of and directed him to 'look to Jesus' the Saviour. Service in the tent again in the evening. ... Oh, what a happy day this has been!... I must now conclude, as I must get ready for the trenches."

On 12th January he wrote: "I have just returned from a night in the trenches, having come off the sick list yesterday morning. Last Sunday I was unable to leave my tent, but I had happy communion with Jesus in my

F. J. Cross

solitude, and derived much pleasure from the fourteenth and fifteenth of St. John. How true is the peace of mind that cleaving to Christ brings to a man! There is nothing like it in this world."

Such was Hedley Vicars - a bright, loving, faithful Christian. He knew what it was to be without peace; for having got into debt when he was first in the army, and knowing the distress it caused his family at home, his mind was so troubled that he wrote to his mother: "Oh, what agony I have endured! What sleepless nights I have passed since the perusal of that letter! The review of my past life, especially the retrospect of the last two years, has at last quite startled me, and at the same time disgusted me." And again: "Oh, that I had the last two years allotted to me to live over again!"

His mother's letters stirred him to sorrow for past faults and desires to live a new life. The sudden death of his fellow-officer, Lieut. Bindon, made him realise the uncertainty of earthly things.

In November, 1851, whilst at Halifax, Nova Scotia, he was awaiting the return of a brother-officer to his room, and idly turning over the leaves of a Bible that was upon the table. He caught sight of the words, "The blood of Jesus Christ His Son cleanseth us from all sin". The message went home. That night he hardly slept. With the morning came LIGHT AND LIFE. Like Christian in the *Pilgrim's Progress* he looked to the cross, and his burden rolled away.

Feeling keenly his own weakness he bought a large Bible, and placed it open on the table in his sitting-room, determined that an open Bible in the future should be his colours. "It was to speak for me," he said, "before I was strong enough to speak for myself." The usual result followed. His friends did not like his "new colours". One accused him of "turning Methodist," and departed; another warned him not to become a hypocrite, and remarked, "Bad as you were, I never thought you would come to this, old fellow!" So for a time he was nearly deserted.

But he had got that which was better than any ordinary friendships. Though he often came under the fire of jeers and taunts - more trying to most men than the rifle bullets of the enemy - he experienced a new joy which increased and deepened.

Later on he would spend four or five hours daily in Bible reading, meditation and prayer, so that whereas he had written a few months earlier: "Oh! dear mother, I wish I felt more what I write!" he was now daily becoming more earnest, patient and watchful, and was gradually putting on the whole armour of God.

And so, during those three short years that intervened between his call to grace and his death at the early age of thirty, he did the work of a lifetime; and of him it can be truly said (as of many another alluded to in this book) that "he being dead yet speaketh".

THE LASS THAT LOVED THE SAILORS.

THE STORY OF AGNES WESTON.

"I was obliged to go to church, but I was determined not to listen, and oftentimes when the preacher gave out the text I have stopped my ears and shut my eyes that I might neither see nor hear."

Thus writes Agnes Weston of the days of her girlhood. There was therefore a time in the life of this devoted woman when there seemed no prospect of her doing good to any one - to say nothing of the great work she has accomplished in giving a helping hand to our sailors in every part of the world.

However, she got out of this Slough of Despond, and having become convinced of God's love she told the good story to the sick in hospitals, to soldiers and sailors without number, and has done more for the good of Jack Tar afloat and ashore than perhaps any other man or woman.

Her public work commenced at the Bath United Hospital, where in 1868 she visited the patients. These looked forward so eagerly to her helpful conversation that in course of time it was arranged she should give a short Gospel address in each of the men's wards once a week.

One day a man who had met with a terrible accident was brought into the hospital whilst she was there. His case was hopeless, and Miss Weston asked that she might be allowed to speak to him. She whispered to him the text, "God so loved the world"; and, though he gave no sign of taking it in, yet presently, when she repeated it, big tears rolled down his face. The word of comfort had reached him.

Another day she came across a poor fellow with both legs broken; and after a little earnest talk he said, "I've been a bad fellow, but I'll trust Him".

Others she found who had been already influenced by Miss Marsh; and so her task of teaching was made easier.

At the Sunday school she showed so great a genius for taming unruly boys that the curate handed over to her the very worst of the youths, that she might "lick them into shape".

Ere long the boys' class developed into a class for working men, which grew and grew till it reached an average attendance of a hundred.

After that followed temperance work. This is how Miss Weston came to sign the pledge.

She was working hard at meetings for the promotion of the temperance cause when a desperate drunkard, a chimney sweep by trade, came to her at one of the meetings and was going to sign the pledge.

Pausing suddenly he remarked, "If you please, Miss Weston, be you a teetotaler?"

F. J. Cross

"No," she replied; "I only take a glass of wine occasionally, of course in strict moderation." Laying down the pen he remarked he thought he'd do the same. So after this Miss Weston became an out-and-out teetotaler, duly pledged.

She had some experience of good work in the army before she took to the navy. The 2nd Somerset Militia assembled every year for drill; and for their benefit coffee and reading rooms were started and entertainments arranged, Miss Weston taking an active part in their promotion. The soldiers' Bible class which she conducted was well attended; and altogether, as one of the officers remarked, "the men were not like the same fellows" after they had been brought under her influence.

The way Agnes Weston was first introduced to the sailors was singular. She had written to a soldier on board the troopship *Crocodile*, and he showed the letter to a sailor friend, who remarked: "That is good: we poor fellows have no friend. Do you think she would write to me?"

"I am sure she will," replied the soldier; "I will write and ask her."

The good news that there was a kind friend willing to write to them gradually spread; and sailor after sailor wrote to Miss Weston, and their correspondence grew so large that at length she had to print her letters.

Even in the first year she printed 500 copies a month of her letters ("little bluebacks" the sailors called them, on account of the colour of their cover); but before many years had passed as many as 21,000 a month were printed and circulated.

Then the sailor boys wanted a letter all to themselves, saying they could not fully understand the men's bluebacks. Miss Weston could not refuse; so she printed them a letter too; and many a reply she had from the boys, telling her of their trials and difficulties, and the help her letters had been to them.

Before Miss Weston had been long at work she thought it would be useful if she went on board the vessels, and had a chat about temperance with the men.

But there was a good deal of difficulty in the way to begin with. A man would have been allowed readily enough, but a *woman* to invade her Majesty's ships, - it was not to be thought of!

At length Admiral Sir King Hall became interested in the subject. He determined to hear what Miss Weston had to say to the men, and, if he was satisfied that her teaching would benefit them, to assist her in her object. He got together a meeting of dockyard workmen, and asked her to speak to them.

So pleased was he with her address that the word went abroad to all the ships in the harbour: "Don't be afraid to let Miss Weston come on board and speak to your ship's company. I'll stand security for her."

She had some grand audiences on the ships, those she addressed sometimes numbering as many as 500.

One day when she went out to the *Vanguard* that vessel was getting up steam ready to go away, having received sudden orders to put out to sea. But, when the captain heard Miss Weston was there to keep an appointment, he put out the accommodation ladder, took her on board, had the notice piped that she had come to give an address; and soon a crowd of sailors was swarming round her in the upper deck battery, standing, sitting, lying, kneeling - all earnestly listening.

Then the pledge book was brought out and placed on one of the big guns, and about forty signed.

On H.M.S. *Topaze* the grog tub was used as a table for signing the pledge book, one sailor remarking (to the tub): "Sixty odd nails in your coffin to-day, old fellow! If they all hold firm I would not give much for your life."

At the present day on board every ship in the service there is a branch of the Royal Navy Temperance Society, and thus our sailors are being encouraged to become sober as well as gallant men.

Having seen to Jack's welfare afloat, the next thing was to look after him on shore; for though the song says: -

If love's the best of all that can a man befall;
Then Jack's the king of all - for they all love Jack;

yet as a matter of fact there are always sharks on the look-out to cheat and rob Jack whenever he has money in his pocket.

Miss Weston took counsel with some officers in the service, and engaged a room for meetings at Devonport. The first Sunday one boy alone came, and next Sunday not a solitary lad made his appearance; so

Miss Wintz, in whose house she was staying, offered a kitchen as more homely, and tea and cake as an attraction. Soon the audience reached a dozen; then all the chairs were filled, and very soon the meetings became so large that the kitchen would not contain all who came; and then a bigger building was provided.

Of course money was needed to enable Miss Weston to develop her scheme to such an extent. But she just asked in the right way; and before long, from one source and another, a sum of nearly £6000 was subscribed, which bought and fitted up a Sailors' Institute and Rest.

Great was the rejoicing of Jack ashore to have a place where he could thoroughly enjoy himself without fear of being plundered or getting drunk. In fact, so great was the enthusiasm that, the night before the house was to be opened, three sailors presented themselves, and said they had asked for special leave to be ashore that night, that they might be the first to sleep in the building.

It turned out that they were the right sort of jacks; for, when the attendant went round to see if all was safe for the night, he found the three seated together, one of them reading aloud the Bible.

Not only has this home prospered, but similar homes have been founded in other places. In Portsmouth Miss Weston's Sailors' Rest is one of the most noted buildings in the town; whilst the principle that Jack, who fights our battles at sea, and keeps our country prosperous by his labours aboard ship, needs to be made happy when he is ashore is far more fully acknowledged than it used to be.

F. J. Cross

Miss Weston's homes are as bright almost as the sunshine. Cheap and good food, tea and coffee both hot and fresh, plenty of light, lots of periodicals and games; and, for those who wish it, short meetings for prayer and praise.

There is a great deal more to tell about Miss Weston, but my space is short; those, however, who wish to know more will find plenty of information in the little book called *Our Blue Jackets*.

A GREAT COMMANDER ON A FAMOUS BATTLEFIELD

THE DUKE OF WELLINGTON AT WATERLOO.

It was on Sunday, 18th June, 1815, that the famous battle of Waterloo was fought. The British army of 67,600 men and the French army of 72,000 lay on the open field the night before that memorable struggle. It had been a wet and stormy night; at dawn the rain was falling heavily, the ground was saturated, and the troops in the rival armies were thoroughly drenched. About nine o'clock it cleared up, but on account of the rainfall no movement was made by the French till towards twelve o'clock.

On the night of the 17th the Duke of Wellington made every portion of his army take up the position it was to occupy on the following day. He slept a few hours at the village of Waterloo and rose early in the morning to write letters, giving orders what was to be done in case the battle was lost: although he felt sure of winning.

Before leaving the village he saw to the preparation of hospitals for the wounded, and to the arrangements made for the distribution of the reserves of ammunition. Then mounting his favourite charger, Copenhagen, he rode to the positions where his men

F. J. Cross

were posted, and made a careful and thorough inspection. The farm house of Hougoumont, where some of the most furious fighting of the day took place, received his special attention.

Having thus done all that a commander could do to ensure the success of the day, he rode back to the high ground from which he could command a full view of the battle, and with a face calm and serene waited for the French attack.

It was this serenity which had so great an effect on his troops. They knew their great commander, and had confidence in him, and this aided them during that eventful day in holding their positions with that stubborn courage which destroyed all the hopes of the Emperor Napoleon.

At Waterloo for the first time the two greatest commanders of the age met face to face. Here across the valley they watched each other in stern anticipation as the church bells called worshippers together for prayer.

At about half-past eleven Napoleon's troops advanced to the attack; and from this time till six or seven o'clock a series of terrific charges continued to be made by the French, resisted and defeated by the steady bravery of the British and Germans.

The duke was often in the thick of the fight, and in so great danger that his staff advised him for the good of the army to withdraw to a somewhat safer position. Passing one of the squares of grenadiers a shell fell among them, and the duke waited to see the result. Several soldiers were blown to pieces by the bursting of the shell, but Wellington seemed quite unmoved either by the terrible sight or his own danger.

All day long the duke was cool as if he had been riding among his men in Hyde Park. Wherever he went a murmur of "Silence! stand to your front!" was heard, and at his presence men grew steady as on parade.

Again and again commanders told him of the fearful havoc made in the ranks of their brigades, and asked either for support or to be allowed to withdraw their men. They generally received this answer, "It is impossible; you must hold the ground to the last man".

When asked by some of his staff what they should do if he fell, he gave the same answer, "My plan is simply to stand my ground here to the last man".

The duke seemed to bear a charmed life. Every member of his staff but one was during the day either killed or wounded, whilst he escaped unhurt. Wherever the danger seemed greatest there was the duke to be found inspiriting his men, restraining them, or putting fresh heart into them.

"Hard pounding this, gentlemen!" he remarked to a battalion on which the French shells were falling with destructive fury; "but we will try who can pound the longest." "Wait a little longer, my lads," was the duke's reply to the murmur which reached him from some of his troops who had suffered heavily from the French fire and were anxious to charge, "and you shall have your wish."

Once when the fire was concentrated on the spot where he was with his staff he told them to separate a little, so as to afford a less conspicuous mark for the enemy.

At another time, when some German troops hesitated to advance against the French, the duke put himself at their head.

When Napoleon's Old Guard was advancing up the hill, the only sight they could see was the duke and a few mounted officers, till a voice was heard, "Up, guards, and at them!" And the best men in the whole French army, the pick of the bravest of the brave, fell back before the onset of the British guards.

At about eight o'clock the duke gave the joyful signal for an advance all along the line. For nearly nine hours the British had been stormed at with shot and shell, had been charged again and again, and had stood firm though impatient. Now they received the signal with a fierce delight, and dashed forward against the enemy with a fury which nothing could resist.

The duke was amongst the first to advance, and spoke joyously to the men as he rode along. The bullets were whistling around him, and one of his staff ventured to point out to him the terrible danger he was running. "Never mind," said the duke, "let them fire away: the battle's won, and my life is of no consequence now."

About 15,000 men out of Wellington's army were killed or wounded on the day of this great battle. But Europe was saved.

The duke, who appeared so calm and unmoved in battle, thus wrote just afterwards, when the excitement of the conflict was over: "My heart is broken at the terrible loss I have sustained in my old friends and companions and my poor soldiers. Believe me, nothing except a battle lost can be half so melancholy as a battle won."

F. J. Cross

A PRINCE OF PREACHERS.

THE STORY OF JOHN WESLEY.

"I do intend to be more particularly careful of the soul of this child that Thou hast so mercifully provided for than ever I have been, that I may do my endeavour to instil into his mind the principles of Thy true religion and virtue. Lord, give me grace to do it sincerely and prudently, and bless my attempts with good success!"

Thus wrote Susanna Wesley of her son John. The child had been nearly burned to death when he was about six years old in a fire that broke out at the Rectory of Epworth, where John and Charles Wesley and a large family were born.

Mrs. Wesley devoted herself to the training of her children, taught them to cry softly even when they were a year old, and conquered their wills even earlier than that. Her one great object was so to prepare her little ones for the journey of life that they might be God's children both in this world and the next. To that end she devoted all her endeavours.

Is it wonderful that, with her example before their eyes and her fervent prayers to help them, the Wesleys made a mark upon the world?

John Wesley - "the brand plucked out of the burning," as he termed himself - when a boy was remarkable for his piety. At eight his father admitted him to the Holy Communion. He had thus early learned the lesson of self-control; for his mother tells us that having small-pox at this age he bore his disease bravely, "like a man and indeed like a Christian, without any complaint, though he seemed angry at the smallpox when they were sore, as we guessed by his looking sourly at them".

At the age of ten John Wesley went to Charterhouse School. For a long time after he got there he had little to live on but dry bread, as the elder boys had a habit of taking the little boys' meat; but so far from this hurting him he said, in after life, that he thought it was good for his health!

Although he was not at school remarkable for the piety he had shown earlier, yet he never gave up reading his Bible daily and saying his prayers morning and evening.

At the age of twenty-two he began to think of entering the ministry, and wrote to his parents about it. He also commenced to regulate the whole tone of his life. "I set apart," he writes, "an hour or two a day for religious retirement; I communicated every week; I watched against all sin, whether in word or deed. I began to aim at and pray for inward holiness." In September, 1725, when he had just passed his twenty-second year, he was ordained.

Thirteen years later John Wesley began that series of journeys to all parts of the kingdom for the purpose of preaching the Gospel, which continued for over

F. J. Cross

half a century.

In that time it is said that he travelled 225,000 miles, and preached more than 40,000 sermons - an average of more than two for every day of the year.

As to the numbers who flocked to hear some of his addresses they can best be realised by those who have attended an international football match, when 20,000 persons are actually assembled in one field, or at a review, when a like number of people are together. It seems impossible to realise that one voice could reach such a multitude; yet it is a fact that some of John Wesley's open-air congregations consisted of over 20,000 persons.

Those were the early days of Methodism, when Whitefield and Wesley were preaching the Gospel, and giving it a new meaning to the multitude.

Here is Wesley's record of one day's work: "May, 1747, Sunday, 10. - I preached at Astbury at five, and at seven proclaimed at Congleton Cross Jesus Christ our wisdom and righteousness and sanctification and redemption. It rained most of the time that I was speaking; but that did not hinder abundance of people from quietly attending. Between twelve and one I preached near Macclesfield, and in the evening at Woodly-green."

His addresses were so fervent that they acted at times like an electric shock. Some would drop down as if thunderstruck, others would cry aloud, whilst others again would have convulsions.

People did not understand such a state of things.

Bishop Butler, author of the *Analogy of Religion*, was ill pleased at a style of preaching so different from that to which the people of the day were accustomed; and told Wesley so.

But the mission of John Wesley was to rouse the masses. This he did, though at great peril to his own life; for his preaching often produced strong opposition.

Thus in June, 1743, at Wednesbury the mob assembled at the house where he was staying, and shouted "Bring out the minister; we will have the minister!" But Wesley was not a bit frightend. He asked that their captain might be brought in to him, and after a little talk the man who came in like a lion went out like a lamb.

Then Wesley went out to the angry crowd, and standing on a chair asked, "What do you want with me?"

"We want you to go with us to the justice!" cried some.

"That I will, with all my heart," he replied.

Then he spoke a few words to them; and the people shouted: "The gentleman is an honest gentleman, and we will spill our blood in his defence".

But they changed their minds later on; for they met a Walsall crowd on their way, who attacked Wesley savagely, and those who had been loud in their promises to protect him - fled!

Left to the mercy of the rable, he was dragged to Walsall. One man hit him in the mouth with such force

F. J. Cross

that the blood streamed from the wound; another struck him on the breast; a third seized him and tried to pull him down.

"Are you willing," cried Wesley, "to hear me?"

"No, no!" they answered; "knock out his brains, down with him, kill him at once!"

"What evil," asked Wesley, "have I done? Which of you all have I wronged by word or deed?" Then he began to pray; and one of the ringleaders said to him: -

"Sir, I will spend my life for you; follow me, and no one shall hurt a hair of your head."

Others took his part also - one, fortunately, being a prizefighter.

Wesley thus describes the finish of this remarkable adventure: -

"A little before ten o'clock God brought me safe to Wednesbury, having lost only one flap of my waistcoat, and a little skin from one of my hands. From the beginning to the end I found the same presence of mind as if I had been sitting in my own study. But I took no thought from one moment to another; only once it came into my mind that, if they should throw me into the river, it would spoil the papers that were in my pocket. For myself I did not doubt but I should swim across, having but a thin coat and a light pair of shoes."

At Pensford the rabble made a bull savage, and then tried to make it attack his congregation; at Whitechapel they drove cows among the listeners and threw stones, one of which hit Wesley between the eyes; but after he had wiped away the blood he went on with his address, telling the people that "God hath not given us the spirit of fear".

At St. Ives in Cornwall there was a great uproar, but Wesley went amongst the mob and brought the chief mischiefmaker out. Strange to say, the preacher received but one blow, and then he reasoned the case out with the agitator, and the man undertook to quiet his companions.

Thus Wesley went fearlessly from place to place. He visited Ireland forty-two times, as well as Scotland and Wales. When he was eighty-four he crossed over to the Channel Islands in stormy weather; and there "high and low, rich and poor, received the Word gladly".

He always went on horseback till quite late in life, when his friends persuaded him to have a chaise. No weather could stop him from keeping his engagements. In 1743 he set out from Epworth to Grimsby; but was told at the ferry he could not cross the Trent owing to the storm.

But he was determined his Grimsby congregation should not be disappointed; and he so worked on the boatmen's feelings that they took him over even at the risk of their lives.

At Bristol, in 1772, he was told that highwaymen were on the road, and had robbed all the coaches that passed, some just previously. But Wesley felt no uneasiness, "knowing," as he writes, "that God would take care of us; and He did so, for before we came to the spot all the highwaymen were taken, and so we went on unmolested, and came safe to Bristol".

This immense labour had no ill effect upon his health. In June, 1786, when he was entering his eighty-fourth year, he writes: "I am a wonder to myself. It is now twelve years since I have felt such a sensation as weariness. I am never tired either with writing, preaching, or travelling."

When Wesley was on his death-bed he wrote to Wilberforce cheering him in his struggle against the slave trade.

"Unless God has raised you up for this very thing," writes Wesley, "you will be worn out by the opposition of men and devils, but if God be for you who can be against you?... Go on in the name of God and in the power of His might till even American slavery, the vilest that ever saw the sun, shall vanish away before it."

Wesley died, at the ripe age of eighty-eight, in the year 1791. He had saved no money, so had none to leave behind; but he was one of those "poor" persons who "make many rich".

Amongst his few small gifts and bequests was "£6 to be divided among the six poor men named by the assistant who shall carry my body to the grave; for I particularly desire that there be no hearse, no coach, no escutcheon, no pomp".

SOME CHILDREN OF THE KINGDOM.

Shortly after Mwanga, King of Uganda, came to the throne, reports were made to that weak-minded monarch that Mr. Mackay, the missionary, was sending messages to Usoga, a neighbouring State, to collect an army for the purpose of invading Uganda. His mind having thus become inflamed with suspicion, he was ready to believe anything against the missionaries, or to invent something if necessary. Thus he complained that his pages, who received instruction from the missionaries, had adopted Jesus as their King, and regarded himself as little better than a brother.

Not long after, six boys were sent to prison; and, though every effort was made to obtain their release, it was for a time of no avail. At length three were given up, and three were ordered to be executed.

These latter were first tortured, then their arms were cut off; afterwards they were placed on a scaffold, under which a fire was made, and burned to death.

As they were passing through their agony, they were laughed at by the people, who asked them if Jesus Christ could do anything to help them.

But the boys were undaunted; and, in spite of all their pain and suffering, sang hymns of praise till their

F. J. Cross

tongues could utter no more. This was one of their hymns: -

Daily, daily, sing to Jesus,
Sing my soul His praises due,
All He does deserves our praises,
And our deep devotion too.

Little wonder that Mr. Mackay should write: "Our hearts are breaking". Yet what a triumph! One of the executioners, struck by the extraordinary fortitude of the lads, and their evident faith in another life, came and asked that he might also be taught to pray. This martyrdom did not daunt the other Christians. Though Mwanga threatened to burn alive any who frequented the mission premises, or adopted the Christian faith, they continued to come; and the lads at the Court kept their teachers constantly informed of everything that was going on. Indeed, when the king's prime minister began to make investigation, he found the place so honey-combed by Christianity that he had to cease his inquisition, for fear of implicating chiefs, and upsetting society generally.

A BOY HERO.

THE STORY OF JOHN CLINTON.

Lives of great men all remind us
We should make our lives sublime,
And departing leave behind us
Footprints on the sands of time.

So sang Longfellow! Yet how difficult is it for most men and women to make their lives sublime, and how much more difficult for a child of ten years! Still it is possible.

John Clinton was born on the 17th January, 1884, at Greek Street, Soho. His father is a respectable carman, who, a year after little Johnnie's birth, moved to 4 Church Terrace, Waterloo Road, Lambeth. When three years old he was sent to the parish schools of St. John's, Waterloo Road (Miss Towers being the mistress). While a scholar there he met with a severe accident on the 27th January, 1890. Playing with other children in the Waterloo Road, a heavy iron gate fell on him and fractured his skull terribly. He was taken to the St. Thomas's Hospital, where he remained for thirteen weeks. At first the doctors said he would not get over it, then that if he got over it he would be an idiot; but finally their surgical skill and careful nursing were rewarded, and he came out well in every respect,

F. J. Cross

except for an awful scar along one side of his head. In due time he moved into the Boys' School at St. John's, Waterloo Road (Mr. Davey, headmaster). In July, 1893, a tiny child was playing in the middle of Stamford Street when a hansom cab came dashing along over the smooth wood paving. Little John Clinton darted out and gave the child a violent push, at the risk of being run over himself, and got the little one to the side of the road in safety. A big brother of the child, not understanding what had happened, gave John Clinton a blow on the nose for interfering with the child, whose life John Clinton had saved. The blow was the cause of this act of bravery becoming known, and the big brother afterwards apologised for his hasty conduct. How many accidents to children are caused by the lamentable absence of open spaces and playgrounds! 460 persons are yearly killed in the streets of London and over 2000 injured there, many of them being children playing in the only place they have to play in.

On Sunday, 26th February, 1893, Johnnie was at home minding the baby. During his temporary absence from the room the baby set itself on fire. When he came back and saw the flames, instead of wasting time calling for help, he rolled the baby on the floor, and succeeded in putting the flames out. The curtain nearest the cot had also taken fire. Johnnie then, though badly burnt, pulled the curtains, valance, and all down on to the floor, and beat out the flames with his hands and feet. The brave little fellow seriously hurt himself, but saved the baby's life, and prevented the buildings catching fire, crowded as they are with other families.

The family then moved to Walworth, 51 Brandon

Street, and the boy attended the schools of St. John's, Walworth (Mr. Ward, headmaster). On the 18th July, 1894, he came home from school, had his tea, and about 5:30 p.m. went out with a companion, Campbell Mortimer, to the foreshore near London Bridge. Here the two boys took off their shoes and stockings, and commenced paddling in the stream. Little Mortimer, unfortunately, got out of his depth, and the tide running strongly he disappeared in the muddy water. Directly the boy came to the surface, John Clinton sprang at him, seized him, and, though Mortimer was the heavier lad of the two, succeeded in landing him safely. In pushing the boy on shore, John Clinton slipped back, and, being exhausted with his exertions, the tide caught him and he disappeared beneath the surface, and was carried down stream a few yards under the pier. The river police dragged for him, and the lightermen did all they could for some considerable time, but without success. After fifteen minutes' fruitless search, a lighterman suggested that the boy must be under the pier. He rowed his boat to the other end of the stage, and there saw the boy's hand upright in the water. He soon got the body out, but life was extinct, and the doctor could only pronounce him to be dead. Thus died John Clinton, a boy of whom London ought to be proud, giving his life for his friend. He was buried in a common grave, at Manor Park Cemetery, after a funeral service in St. John's Church, Walworth.

[*For the above account I am indebted to the Rev. Arthur W. Jephson, M.A., Vicar of St. John's, Walworth.*]

POSTSCRIPT.

For those who desire to learn more of the characters mentioned in this work let me mention a few volumes. In *Heroes of Every-day Life* Miss Laura Lane has told briefly the story of Alice Ayres and other humble heroes and heroines whose deeds should not be forgotten. Further particulars of the careers of Sir Colin Campbell, John Cassell, General Gordon, Sir Henry Havelock, Joseph Livesey, David Livingstone, Robert Moffat, George Moore, Florence Nightingale, Lord Shaftesbury, Agnes Weston, and other men and women whose example has benefited the country, will be found in an attractive series of books issued under the title of *The World's Workers*. Mr. Archibald Forbes' *Life of Sir Henry Havelock* is one of the most fascinating works of its kind; the Rev. H.C.G. Moule's *Life of the Rev. Charles Simeon* is delightfully written and full of interest, and the Rev. J.H. Overton's *Life of Wesley* gives an admirable picture in brief of the great revival preacher. Further particulars of the great and good Father Dainien can be gathered from Mr. Edward Clifford's work; of Elizabeth Gilbert, from the Life by Frances Martin; and of George Müller, from the shilling autobiography he has written, which is worthy of the deepest attention. John Howard's life has been well told by Mr. Hepworth Dixon, Lord Shaftesbury's by Mr. Edwin Hodder, and Mr. Glaisher's career is set forth at large in *Travels in the Air*. Perhaps the largest and best collection of narratives of noble lives is contained in Mr. Edwin Hodder's *Heroes of Britain in Peace and War*, now issued in two cheap volumes; from this many facts have been gathered. In *The Memorials of Captain Hedley Vicars* will be found a thoughtful picture of that devoted life; whilst in *The Life and Work of James Hannington*, by E.C. Dawson, a graphic narrative is given of the martyr bishop of Central Africa. *Ismailia* affords a vivid picture of Sir Samuel Baker's life in the Soudan, and few books will give greater pleasure to the reader than General Butler's *Life of General Gordon*. A Life of Mr. W.H. Smith, by Sir H. Maxwell, has been recently published in popular form. *The Lives of Robert and Mary Moffat*, by J.S. Moffat, will afford much enjoyment, as will Miss Yonge's *Life of Bishop Patteson*.

F. J. Cross